THE GUNSMITH

485

The Central City Poker Challenge

Books by J.R. Roberts
(Robert J. Randisi)

The Gunsmith series

Gunsmith Giant series

Lady Gunsmith series

Angel Eyes series

Tracker series

Mountain Jack Pike series

COMING SOON!
The Gunsmith
486 – The Runaway Wife

For more information
visit: www.SpeakingVolumes.us

THE GUNSMITH

485

The Central City Poker Challenge

J.R. Roberts

SPEAKING VOLUMES, LLC
NAPLES, FLORIDA
2023

The Central City Poker Challenge

Copyright © 2023 by Robert J. Randisi

ISBN 979-8-89022-012-7

Chapter One

Clint Adams rode into Blackhawk, Colorado on his way to Central City, which was another hundred miles north. There was a poker game waiting for him in Central City, but he felt his Tobiano could use a rest and, truth be told, he was kind of tired himself. So before taking a hundred-mile trek to Central City which, if he pushed, would still be two or three nights on the trail, he thought he and his buddy, Toby, would take a short blow.

He got his horse and himself settled and stopped in a small cafe for a meal. The hotel he chose didn't have dining services, which was fine with him. It was small and comfortable otherwise.

He dined on beef stew and beer, paid his bill and stepped out on the street. Walking for a spell, he found many of the town businesses closing for the day, even though it was only four p.m.

One man was sweeping up in front of his store, a leather shop. As Clint approached, the man stopped and leaned on his broom. He was in his sixties, wearing a long white apron.

"Howdy," the man said.

" 'afternoon," Clint said.

"Just get to town?"

"A little while ago. Kind of early for the town to close up, isn't it?"

"That's the way it's been since the theater opened."

"Theater?" Clint asked. "When did that happen?"

"A few months ago," the man said. "Some theater people came to town, decided to set up here. Bought a building, started putting on shows. Folks went to their shows, which meant they wouldn't come here or to other shops in the afternoon. Then shop owners started closin' early to go to the shows themselves. Pretty soon we all just started closing at four."

"How long do you think this'll go?" Clint wondered.

"Who knows?" the man said. "From what I hear, they're openin' a theater up in Central City, as well."

"Is it going to be as popular there?"

"Who knows?" the man said. "They've already got an opera house."

"Looks like this is going to become theater country," Clint said.

"I hope not. We don't need them kind of people in the West. I'm hopin' they'll give up and go back East where they belong."

"Do many of the other storekeepers feel the same?" Clint asked.

"The ones my age do," the man said, "but we got lots of new folks since the mines started givin' out."

Blackhawk had been a mining town for a long time, but Clint hadn't heard of them giving out.

"All the mines are dry?" he asked.

"Naw, some of the old ones are still active, but there ain't been a new strike in a month of Sundays. The new citizens ain't miners, they're ranchers and storekeepers. And, oh yeah, those theater folk."

"Where's this theater?" Clint asked.

"Coupla streets down," the man said. "Useta be a warehouse. And there's talk about building a new one."

"Well," Clint said, "I won't be here long. I'm heading for Central City."

"Good luck," the man said. "They're gettin' all fancified, too."

"I'm goin' to a poker game," Clint said, "so there's nothing fancy about that."

"Like I said, good luck," the man said, sniffed, and went into his store. He slammed the door and locked it.

Clint continued walking. He understood the man's feelings about the theaters. He himself disliked the number of eastern style police stations that were popping up in the West and pushing sheriffs and town marshals out of jobs. He was starting to feel pretty long in the tooth as people looked at him as part of the dying Old West.

Within a few blocks he saw the large building looming up ahead of him. There had been an attempt to whitewash the word WAREHOUSE off the side, without complete success. When he reached the building, he saw that a handmade marquee had been erected over the front door with the word THEATER on it, in capital letters.

As he got close to the front door beneath the marquee, he saw some posters with the names of the performers who were appearing. As you would expect, there was a "songbird," a lovely young lady singer and an actor, doing Shakespeare. But there was also a man who did card tricks and—most interesting to Clint—a trick shooter.

It looked like he was going to the theater, tonight.

Chapter Two

Clint didn't understand this new 4 o'clock closing time for the merchants, since the starting time for the theater was 7 p.m. All he could figure was that the ladies in town needed a lot of time to get gussied up for a night of entertainment.

According to the poster, the singer went on at 7, the actor 8, the card shark 9 and the trick shot artist at 10. That meant Clint had plenty of time to have a bath and a haircut, and then dress for the theater. He might even have had time for a steak.

He had no idea what was going on inside the theater at that moment . . .

***

E.P. Milton managed not only the theater, but all the acts. He had come west to bring theater to the filthy masses of miners and cowboys. He was sitting in his office, examining the paperwork that reflected his investment not only in Blackhawk, but Central City, as well.

He looked up from his desk only when there was a knock at the door.

"Come in!" he snapped, sitting back in his chair.

His assistant, Jack de Lancie entered. He had brought the younger man with him when he came west, and the man had adapted very nicely. He wore Western garb, and the only thing missing from his ensemble was a gun. But de Lancie had no idea how to use a gun and letting him carry one was just an accident waiting to happen.

"What is it, Jack?"

"I heard something, and I've managed to confirm it," de Lancie said.

"And what's that?"

"Clint Adams is in town."

"Why do I know that name?" Milton asked, rubbing his jaw.

"He's the Gunsmith."

"That's it!" Milton snapped. "Do you think we can get him into the theater?"

"I happen to know he bought a ticket for tonight."

"Where are you getting this information?"

"The clerk in his hotel."

"Is he in the Palace?"

"No," de Lancie said, "a small hotel called The Sunrise. Doesn't even have a dining room."

"What's he doing there?"

de Lancie shrugged and said, "Keeping a low profile, I imagine."

"This is interesting," Milton said, "very interesting."

"What do you want me to do?"

"I want you to make sure he gets a good seat," Milton said.

"I don't know when he's coming or what he wants to see," de Lancie said.

"Then wait for him," Milton said.

"Wait . . . you mean, at the box office?"

"Where else?"

"But I don't know what time he's coming."

"Then you wait there until he does come," Milton said. "You tell him we're honored by his presence and take him to a good seat."

"Up front?"

"In a box, Jack, with a good view."

"Okay," de Lancie said, "and then what?"

"Then tell him that I'd like to meet him."

"Tonight?"

"No," Milton said, "tell him in the morning, for breakfast."

"And if he says no?"

Milton leaned his elbows on the desk.

"You don't let him say no," he said. "Tell him it'll be very interesting."

"I'll do my best."

"You do that."

de Lancie stood up and asked, "Breakfast where, sir?"

"Where do I usually have breakfast, Jack?"

"Right, right."

"I'll be here during all the performances," Milton said. "When you get him seated, you let me know."

"Yes, sir."

"Now go," Milton said. "I have some paperwork to review on the Central City theater."

"I thought you wanted to take over the opera house?" de Lancie asked.

"I haven't made my mind up yet," Milton said. "We could still build our own theater."

"That'll be expensive—"

"I don't need you to tell me that, Jack," Milton snapped. "Now go and do your job."

"Yes, sir."

As usual, Jack de Lancie left his boss's office, feeling angry and disrespected.

E.P. Milton sat back in his chair and ignored the paperwork on his desk. Having The Gunsmith in Blackhawk put an entire new spin on things.

Chapter Three

After a bath and change of clothes, Clint asked the desk clerk for a likely place to get a steak.

"You can get a steak in a few places," the young man said. "But if you want a good one, you'll have to go across town to the Theater Club."

"The Theater Club?"

"It's a place that opened in the last six months, since the theater opened. A lot of people go there for supper, before or after the performances."

"I see."

"They brought in a chef from New York," the clerk went on. "Just havin' a cook wasn't good enough for them."

"Tell me," Clint said, "do the same people who own the theater also own the restaurant?"

"The same person," the clerk said. "His name's E.P. Milton. He came from New York."

"Ah," Clint said. "Well, a steak is a steak. Thanks."

"Yes, sir. Enjoy your dinner."

"I think I will."

Clint left the hotel and decided to walk across town to the restaurant. It was that pleasant a night . . .

***

When he reached the Theater Club he wondered if he was going to have to be a member to get in. But when he presented himself at the door, he was welcomed in and shown to a table by a bow tie wearing waiter.

"Would you like to see a menu, sir?"

"I've been told you do the best steak in town," Clint said.

"You were told correctly, sir."

"I'll have that, then."

"With a cold beer?" the waiter asked. "It's the best way to eat it."

"Definitely a cold beer. Thanks."

"Yes, sir. Coming up."

Clint sat back and looked around. Almost every table was occupied, mostly with people who looked as if they had dressed for the theater. All Clint had done was put on a clean shirt. He didn't take the time to go out and buy a new suit just for the night.

The waiter returned with a large, frothy glass mug of cold beer, and a huge steak surrounded by vegetables.

"Enjoy, sir."

"Thank you."

He picked up his knife and fork and went to work . . .

***

E.P. Milton was sitting at his usual table, in a corner. He put down his knife and fork and waved the waiter over.

"Yes, sir?"

"Gary," Milton said," who is that gentleman sitting at table ten?"

"I don't know, sir. I've never seen him before."

"So he's a stranger in town."

"He's a stranger here, certainly," Gary said. "Would you like me to ask him his name?"

Milton thought a moment, then said, "No, that's fine. Go back to work."

"Yes, sir."

Milton figured he was going to see the Gunsmith in the theater soon enough. He would find out then if it was the same man. He went back to his meal, which was a vcal dish, the recipe for which had come directly from New York.

E.P. Milton missed New York, but it wouldn't be healthy for him to go back there.

Clint had a sixth sense for when somebody in a room was interested in him. Looking around at the other diners, he saw that he had come to the attention of a man seated alone. Then, after the waiter served him his food, he saw the man call the waiter over and speak to him. Clint knew they were discussing him.

When the waiter came to collect his plate he asked, "How was your steak, sir?"

"It was excellent, thank you."

"Would you like dessert?"

"I'm going to your new theater in town," Clint said, "but I suppose I have time. What do you have?"

"We have a large variety of pies and cakes, sir."

"Peach pie?"

"Yes, sir."

"Good. I'll have a large slice and a cup of coffee."

"How would you like the coffee, sir?"

"Strong and black, please."

"Of course, sir," the waiter said. "Just as you like."

While he waited for his dessert, the man at the corner table finished his meal, stood and left, without paying.

"When the waiter returned he said, "Can you tell me who the man at that corner table was?"

"Sir?"

"Seems to me he asked you about me."

"Oh, yes sir," the waiter said. "That was Mr. Milton."

"E.P. Milton?"

"Yes, sir. He owns the restaurant."

"And the theater, I hear."

"Yes, sir."

"And he was interested in me?"

"Well, sir," the waiter said, "he asked me if I knew who you were."

"And do you?"

"No, sir."

"Did he want you to ask me who I was?"

"No, sir."

"All right, thank you."

"Enjoy your pie, sir."

Clint sliced a hunk from the pie and popped it into his mouth. He washed it down with a sip of coffee and thoroughly enjoyed it. In fact, he enjoyed the entire dining experience he'd had in the Theater Club.

Next was a visit to the actual theater.

Chapter Four

Clint was glad he had walked to the Theater Club. This way he was able to walk the meal off on his way to the theater.

While he was interested in seeing the trick shooter perform his act on stage, he actually arrived at the theater in plenty of time to see the card tricks.

He stopped at the box office to pick up his ticket, and as he turned to enter, a young man stepped in front of him . . .

***

Jack de Lancie had been waiting at the box office since six o'clock, not wanting to risk missing the Gunsmith. de Lancie had contacts in many of the hotels in town, so that he might be told whenever someone of note checked in. It took only a few coins to get the young desk clerk at Clint's hotel on his contact list. Now he waited for a man fitting the description he had gotten from the clerk to arrive. Seven went by, and then eight, but finally he saw a likely match come to the box office before nine.

"Sir?" he said, stepping in the man's way as he turned to go into the theater.

"Yes?"

"I'm sorry, sir," de Lancie said, "but are you Clint Adams?"

"Who's asking?" Clint asked.

"My name is Jack de Lancie. I work for the theater."

"Ah, then that means you work for Mr. Milton."

"Oh, yes," de Lancie said, surprised. "Do you know Mr. Milton?"

"No, but I've heard of him," Clint said. "In fact, I just came from the Theater Club, where he and I had dinner—separately, of course."

"Yes, he eats his dinner there every night."

"What can I do for you, Mr. de Lancie?"

"It's what I can do for you, sir," de Lancie said. "I want to make sure you have a good seat. If you'd follow me?"

"Well, thank you."

Clint followed the young man into the theater and up some steps to the second level. They walked past several curtained doorways until they reached one near the front.

"Right here, sir," de Lancie said, holding the curtain back.

Clint stepped through the doorway into a box that afforded him a wonderful view of the stage below.

"Is this satisfactory, sir?" de Lancie asked.

"It's fine, thank you," Clint said. "I didn't expect such service."

"Did you arrive in time to see the card tricks, deliberately?"

"No, it's just that I finished my dinner and came right over. I actually wanted to see the trick shooter."

"Ah yes, of course," de Lancie said. "Kit is very good."

"I hope so," Clint said. "I'm looking forward to it."

"Well, have a seat and enjoy the show."

"Thank you."

Clint wondered how E.P. Milton had figured out who he was at the restaurant, and gotten word to the theater so quickly?

The man on the stage was in the middle of a card trick, so Clint watched without knowing what the setup had been. He then saw the rest of the performance, and applauded on cue when the act was finished and the curtain drawn.

He waited patiently for the curtain to open again. A young man wearing a tuxedo came out and introduced the trick shooter, Kit Dalton.

Clint was surprised when a woman came out on stage, wearing a pistol and carrying a rifle.

Chapter Five

The only lady sharpshooter Clint had ever seen was Annie Oakley, who performed with Buffalo Bill's Wild West Show.

That was, until today.

Kit Dalton stood at the end of the stage nearest to Clint, but with her back to him. That was all he saw of her. Targets were set up at the other end. She took care of some of them with her pistol, and others with her rifle. She never hesitated, didn't seem to aim, and never missed. She seemed to be a natural shot—with targets. When you're a natural you don't need to aim, you simply point.

Clint had seen a few natural shots over the years. His friend Wild Bill Hickok, Bat Masterson, Ben Thompson and—the only other lady—Roxy Doyle.

And now Kit Dalton, although there was a big difference between shooting at targets and shooting at men.

Kit Dalton moved to the center of the stage to take her bows. When she turned to leave the stage, Clint could see that she was very pretty and fairly young.

Clint was about to step from the box when Jack de Lancie came through the curtain.

"So what did you think, Mr. Adams?" he asked.

"That Kit Dalton is pretty good."

"Pretty good?" de Lancie asked. "She never misses."

"Yes," Clint said. "She never misses. But she's shooting at stationary targets."

"Well, for moving targets we'd have to take the show outside," de Lancie said.

"Maybe that's something you should think about," Clint said. "Or talk to your boss about."

"Since you mentioned my boss," de Lancie said, "Mr. Milton would like it if you would join him for breakfast in the morning."

"Is that so?" Clint asked. "What's he got in mind?"

"He doesn't tell me that."

"And where would this breakfast take place?"

"Well, Mr. Milton takes all his meals at the Theater Club," de Lancie explained.

"And what time does he have breakfast?"

"Every morning at seven forty-five."

"Hmm, that's pretty early."

"I'm sure I could get him to meet you at eight," de Lancie said.

"That sounds better."

"Meanwhile, would you like to come backstage and meet the performers?"

"I don't think so," Clint said. "I'm going to head right back to my hotel. I might stop along the way somewhere for a drink. Good night, Mr. de Lancie."

Clint left de Lancie standing there, feeling unsure of himself. He went down the stairs and left the theater before the man could recover.

***

After Clint Adams left, Jack de Lancie went to his boss's office.

"Well," Milton asked.

"He watched the card tricks and Kit's shooting."

"Was he impressed?"

"Not so much," de Lancie said. "He said she was shooting at stationary targets."

"Did he go backstage and meet her?"

"No," de Lancie said, "he didn't want to. After the show he just left."

Milton thought a moment, then asked, "What'd he look like." He listened while de Lancie described the Gunsmith. "Okay, yeah, that was him I saw at dinner in the club."

"He said he saw you there."

"Really? I guess he knew I was watching him and wondering. What about breakfast tomorrow?

"He said, sure, but at eight."

"I'll be there at my usual time," Milton said. "I don't care what time he shows up, I just want to talk to him."

"Well, he'll be there."

"Fine," Milton said. "You can go, now."

"Good night sir," de Lancie said, and left.

***

Clint found a saloon called The Colony, and hoped it had no connection to the theater crowd. As it turned out, most of the clientele looked like miners and ranch hands.

He went to the bar, where he had to elbow himself some room, and ordered a beer. Nobody seemed to mind him edging himself in.

He took his beer and turned to look the place over. There were no table games, and only one girl working the floor. The atmosphere was sleepy. All these folks seemed to have come there after a day's work.

Clint finished his beer and went back to his hotel. This place had made him feel sleepy, as well.

Chapter Six

In the morning Clint left his hotel and again walked to the Theater Club.

"I'm meeting Mr. Milton for breakfast," he told the host.

"Yes, sir. This way."

He followed the man to the same corner table he had seen Milton at the night before.

"Your guest, sir," the host said.

Milton stood and extended his hand.

"Mr. Adams, a pleasure to meet you. I was told you would be coming later."

"I was told you ate breakfast at seven forty-five. I didn't want to keep you waiting."

"I appreciate that," Milton said. "Have a seat, please."

Clint sat across from the man. Milton looked to be in his forties, with an impressive head of brown/grey hair, and a pale complexion.

"What would you like for breakfast?" Milton asked.

"I'll have whatever you're having."

"Good." He waved at the waiter and held up two fingers.

Clint looked around, saw that every table was occupied.

"What did you think of our show last night?" Milton asked.

"Very entertaining."

"And Kit?" Milton asked. "Did she impress you?"

"She's a very good shot," Clint said, "but a lot of people can shoot at stationary targets."

"Yes, de Lancie told me you said that. Is there a way we can have moving targets on stage?"

"I don't think shooting should be done inside," Clint said. "If she shot outside, you could do a lot more."

"Well, when I build a new theater, I'll make sure there's an open area."

The waiter came with their breakfast.

"Omelets," Milton said. "Have you had them before?"

"I have, a time or two."

"Out west?"

"I've been to New York."

"Have you? For what reason?"

"Several," Clint said, "but one time I was there to see my friend, P.T. Barnum."

Milton looked shocked.

"You know P.T. Barnum?"

"I do."

"And what about Annie Oakley?"

"A good friend of mine."

"Kit would love to hear that," Milton said. "Would you meet her?"

"If you like," Clint said, "but it'd have to be soon. I'm leaving for Central City."

"I'm considering building a theater there, you know," Milton said.

"I hear they already have an opera house," Clint said.

"Do you like opera?" Milton asked.

"Not really," Clint said. "I don't understand it."

"I don't either," Milton said. "But I believe a theater would work well there."

"I wish you luck," Clint said.

"Why are you going there?" Milton asked.

"To play poker."

"Ah, you're a gambler."

"In more ways than one," Clint said.

"Maybe we should talk again in Central City," Milton said. "I have some ideas."

"Why would we talk again?"

"Because some of my ideas might concern you," Milton said.

"I probably wouldn't be interested," Clint told him.

"Why don't we wait and see?" Milton said. "Meanwhile, how about meeting Kit tonight after her performance?"

"In the theater?"

Milton nodded and said, "Backstage."

"I don't see why not," Clint agreed.

From that point on they paid attention to their breakfast.

***

After breakfast Milton had the waiter bring another pot of coffee.

"I understand you like it hot, strong and black."

"This is very good," Clint said, "but I guess I should be going."

"I'll walk out with you," Milton said. "My office is at the theater."

The two men walked out together. There was a buggy waiting for Milton.

"Can I give you a ride to your hotel?" he asked Clint.

"No, that's okay," Clint said. "I'd rather walk."

"Then I'll see you tonight at the theater," Milton said, getting into the buggy. "I'll leave a ticket for you at the box office."

"Thanks," Clint said. "I'll see you then."

He watched Milton's buggy ride away, then started walking to his hotel.

Chapter Seven

This time Clint arrived at the theater early enough to see all the acts.

Once again, de Lancie met him out front, but this time Clint insisted on seating himself.

"As you wish, but I'll collect you afterward to take you backstage."

"Fine," Clint said.

He entered the theater and found himself a seat amongst all the others in the audience. He was prepared to sit through four hours of entertainment. Why not? He wasn't leaving for Central City until morning.

The woman who came out to sing was very good. The actor doing Shakespeare was a bit overblown. The man who did the card tricks was very skilled, and Clint had no idea how he did them. And then came Kit Dalton, who was very smooth and competent.

When the show was over and the theatergoers were filing out, Clint remained in his seat. Eventually, Jack de Lancie came to fetch him.

"Ready to meet Kit?" de Lancie asked.

"Lead the way."

He followed de Lancie to the front of the house, where they walked along the stage and through a door to the back.

"Kit's dressing room is this way," de Lancie said.

He led Clint to a closed door, where he knocked.

"Come in," a woman's voice called.

de Lancie opened the door. "Kit, I have Clint Adams here."

"Really?" She had been sitting in front of a mirror, wiping makeup from her face. Now she jumped up. "Oh, my God! The Gunsmith?"

"This is him," de Lancie said.

"It's such a pleasure!" Kit gushed.

Clint couldn't tell when she was on stage that she was about twenty-five and stood five-foot-five. She was still wearing the buckskin jacket she'd worn on stage, with a matching skirt.

"Did you see me shoot?"

"I did," Clint said. "You're very good."

"Do you really think so?" she asked. "Thank you so much. That's such a compliment coming from you. Mr. Milton told me you might come by."

"I just wanted to say how much I enjoyed your show."

"Mr. Milton told me that you're friends with Annie Oakley," Kit said.

"That's true."

"Am I as good as her?"

"Well," Clint said, "it's hard to say after seeing you just twice, but nobody's as good as Annie."

"Including you?"

"I'm not a target shooter," Clint said.

"Of course not," she said. "You're a gunfighter. You kill men."

"That's not the way I'd put it," Clint said.

"Oh!" She put her hands over her mouth. "I didn't mean to insult you. I was just referring to your reputation."

"That's all right," Clint said. "I deal with what people think of me all the time. But now I have to be going."

"I really appreciate your coming to see me, Mr. Adams. It means a lot."

"You're welcome."

"Will you be staying in town much longer?" she asked.

"No, I'll be leaving in the morning."

"Oh, that's too bad," she said. "I wish we could have had a meal together and, you know, gotten better acquainted."

"I'm sorry," he said, "but I'm expected in Central City."

"I'll see if I can find Jack—"

"No need," Clint said. "I'll find my way out. Good-bye, Miss Dalton."

"Goodbye, Mr. Adams."

Clint left the dressing room and made his way out of the theater.

***

When she was sure Clint Adams was gone, Kit Dalton left her dressing room and walked to E.P. Milton's office.

"Come in," he said, when she knocked. "Ah, Kit. Did Clint Adams come to your dressing room?"

"He did," she said, scowling. "I don't think he was very impressed with me."

"Well, he did say something about shooting at stationary targets—"

"I want to shoot against him!" she spat.

"Against the Gunsmith?"

"He wasn't impressed with me, I'm not impressed with him. He's old and worn out."

Milton stared at the girl. At her age, everybody else was old and worn out.

"How do you expect to shoot against him?" he asked.

"He's going to Central City tomorrow," she said. "You're going there, too. Make it happen."

"Kit—"

"Make it happen! Or I'm through!"

She turned and stormed out.

Milton sat back and smiled.

Chapter Eight

In the morning Clint found a small café, had a quick breakfast, then went to the livery to saddle his Tobiano. He rode to a mercantile and bought a few supplies, just enough to get him to Central City. He stowed the supplies in a gunny sack and hung it from his saddle horn. Then he mounted up and rode out of town, heading north.

***

E.P. Milton ate his breakfast slowly and waited. Eventually, Jack de Lancie showed up with another man in tow and came over to the table.

"Sheriff's here, Mr. Milton," he said.

"I can see that, Jack," Milton said. "You can go now."

"Yes, sir."

Milton looked at Sheriff Rufus Candliss. He had been the sheriff of Blackhawk for seven years, and was now fifty years old, and pretty set in his ways. He did not like the direction the town was taking since there were no new mines opening up, but he recognized the amount of authority E.P. Milton had gained in the six months since he came to town, so he treated the man with respect.

"You have breakfast yet, Sheriff?" he asked.

"No, sir, not yet."

"Well then, have a seat and join me."

"Me?" Candliss asked. "Eat breakfast here?"

"Why not?"

"Well," Candliss said, "this just might ruin me for any other place in town."

"I think you deserve a good breakfast once in a while, don't you, Sheriff?"

"Yessir, I do."

"Then take a seat and I'll have the waiter bring you a good breakfast."

Candliss hesitated, then pulled a chair out, sat in it, removed his hat and set it on an empty chair. He knew Milton had something on his mind, and he figured he might as well get a good meal out of whatever it was.

There was a pot of coffee on the table and two empty cups. Milton picked the pot up and poured both cups full.

"Thank ya," Candliss said, picking up one cup.

"Sheriff," Milton said, "do you know who was in town the last two days?"

"I reckon I don't," the lawman said.

"Clint Adams."

"The Gunsmith?" Candliss asked, surprised. "In Blackhawk?"

"That's right."

The waiter came and set a plate of steak-and-eggs in front of the sheriff.

"I figured that's what a man like you would want for breakfast, Sheriff."

"Well, you figured right, Mr. Milton," Sheriff Candliss said, "you figured right." He picked up his knife and fork and cut into the steak. "What was the Gunsmith doing in Blackhawk?" he wondered aloud.

"He said he was on his way to Central City to play in a poker game," Milton said. "Would you know anything about that, Sheriff?"

"Yes, sir," Candliss said, as he chewed, "there's a big game in Central City later this week. Some big-name gamblers are gonna be there."

"I assume there's a telegraph office in Central City," Milton said.

"Yes, sir, there is."

"And you know the sheriff there?"

"I sure do," Candliss said. "His name's Harvey Wood."

"Then maybe you should send Sheriff Wood a telegram and tell him that the Gunsmith is on his way there."

"I could do that."

"And I'd like him to put Adams in jail until I get there," Milton added.

"Put the Gunsmith in jail?" Candliss asked. "On what charge?"

"Charge?"

"You can't just put a man in jail without chargin' him with somethin'."

"Oh, I see," Milton said. "Well, suppose you were to think of something."

"Whataya want him in jail for?" Candliss asked.

"I want the man to feel beholding to me when I get him out."

"So you don't want him in jail for long, huh?"

"Just until I can get there," Milton said. "Is there a stagecoach between here and there?"

"There is," Candliss said. "It should be along later in the week."

"Good," Milton said, "you can tell Sheriff Wood I'll be on that stage."

"I'll do that," Candliss said. He looked down at his plate and asked, "Can I do it after breakfast?"

"By all means," Milton said, "finish your breakfast first, Sheriff."

Happily, the lawman went back to work on his steak.

Chapter Nine

That night Milton waited in his room patiently, until there was a knock on the door. When he opened it Kit Dalton came storming in.

"Did you do it?" she demanded.

"Do what?" he asked.

"Did you get Clint Adams to agree to shoot with me?"

"Kit, he left town."

"Where'd he go?"

"Central City."

"That's not so far," she said. "Go and get him."

"I am going to Central City," he said, "but on business. While I'm there, though, I'll approach him."

"You better," Kit said. "When I outshoot him, I'll have a big name."

"Yes, you will," he said, "and I suppose you'll make me pay for it."

"You bet," she said. "In fact, I may be too big for you. E.P."

"Too big for me to employ, but not too big to, uh—"

"Oh, shut up." she said.

Milton was dressed for bed, wearing silk pajamas. He had brought three pair with him from New York.

Kit approached him, unbuttoned the pajama top and peeled it off him. Then she untied the pajama bottoms and allowed them to fall to the floor. She reached for his flaccid penis and stroked it to life, as Milton was twenty-five years older than her, he needed the assistance. Then she backed away and began to disrobe. Before long, her buckskin garb was on the floor, followed by her under-things, and she was as naked as he was.

She had teacup breasts and slender hips, and skin like alabaster. By this time Milton's cock had risen to full mast. She grabbed hold of it and tugged him to the bed. Once on the bed together, he began to stroke her body with his fingertips and bring her nipples to life with his mouth.

Usually, Kit put up with his ministrations as long as she could and brought him to climax as quickly as she could, but tonight she felt she needed to spend more time with him, and make sure he was grateful enough to find a way to get Clint Adams to shoot with her.

"You'll head for Central City tomorrow morning?" she asked him, holding his head as he licked her breasts.

"Yes, tomorrow."

She lifted his head and looked into his eyes.

"You promise?"

"Yes, I promise."

She scooted down between his legs, began to wet his cock with her tongue before taking it into her mouth and slowly sucking . . .

***

Clint rode into Central City, after spending three nights on the trail. It had been a relaxing time, with the Fall weather cool during the day and cooler in the evenings. When he arrived, he was just about ready for a few days of high stakes poker.

Central City was a smaller town than Blackhawk, and many of the buildings looked newly erected, or repaired. He wondered if the mines here had played out, as well.

His invitation to the poker game—which had a ten thousand dollar buy-in—gave him a choice of two hotels to stay in, each of which had a special rate for poker players. After boarding his horse at the local livery, he chose to check into the Central City Hotel.

"Welcome, sir," the young desk clerk said. "Here for the game?"

"I am." Clint showed the clerk the telegram he had received with the invitation.

"Very good, sir," the clerk said. "Do you have a preference? Main floor? Second floor? Room overlooking the street, or the alley?"

"Not the street," Clint said. "Do the alley rooms have access from outside the window?"

"No, sir," the clerk said. "The windows don't overlook nothin' but the alley, with nothing underneath."

"Then I'll take a room overlooking the alley."

"Yes, sir." The clerk grabbed a key and passed it over. "Room fifteen."

"Thank you."

"Good luck, sir."

"Thanks."

Clint took his saddlebags and rifle up to his room and peered out the window to be sure the clerk had been correct. There was no access from outside. It was a straight drop down to the alley floor.

Clint was about to leave the room, to have a look at the venue for the poker game, when there was a knock at the door.

"Who is it?"

"Sheriff Wood."

Clint opened the door a crack, saw a man with a badge in the hall. He opened the door wide, saw that the man was in his fifties, as tired looking as most lifetime lawmen.

"What can I do for you, Sheriff?" Clint asked.

"Are you Clint Adams, sir?"

"I am."

"Would you come with me to my office?" the sheriff asked. "We need to talk."

"About what?"

"I'll be able to explain better in my office, if you don't mind."

"All right," Clint said. "Lead the way."

***

Clint followed the lawman from the hotel to his office, traveling several streets from the hotel to get there. People they passed along the way looked after them, curiously. Sheriff Wood exchanged nods of greeting with many of them.

When they reached the small sheriff's office, Woods opened the front door with a key, and then led Clint inside.

"Al right," Clint said, "we're here. What's this all about, Sheriff?"

"Just let me open my drawer—" the lawman started, but he came out of the drawer with a gun and pointed it at Clint.

"I'll have to ask you for your gun, Mr. Adams."

"What for?"

"Well, I can't put you in a cell still wearin' it."

"Put me in a cell?" Clint asked. "For what? I just got to town. What law have I broken?"

"No law here in Central City that I know of," Sheriff Wood said, "but I've been asked by the sheriff of Blackhawk to, uh, detain you."

"Again, on what charge?"

"If you insist, Mr. Adams," Wood said, "I'm gonna have to charge you with resisting arrest."

Clint could see that the sheriff was very nervous, so he decided to push the matter.

"I'm afraid I'm not going to be able to go along with this, Sheriff," Clint said. "I don't intend to sit in one of your cells while my poker game goes on without me."

"Mr. Adams—"

"Besides," Clint continued, "if you're going to arrest me, you'll want my gun."

"Well, yeah—"

"Then you're going to have to take it," Clint said, "as I don't intend to give it to you."

Sheriff Wood not only looked nervous, but frustrated.

"Mr. Adams," he said, "I was hopin' you'd be a law abidin' citizen and just gimme your gun."

"That's not going to happen."

"So you're resisting arrest?"

"Definitely."

Sheriff Wood stared at him.

"So unless you're going to take me by force, I'll be on my way."

Wood had nothing to say to that, so Clint left the office and went back to his hotel.

Chapter Ten

In the lobby of his hotel, he asked the desk clerk if he could see the register.

"Certainly, sir," the clerk said, turning the book around.

Clint looked at all the names who had registered before him. He recognized some of them, but didn't see anyone he would call a friend. He was hoping Bat Masterson might be there, so they could share a meal.

"If you don't see who you're looking for sir," the clerk said, "they might be in the other hotel."

"That's the Dundee, isn't it?"

"Right."

"I'll check there. Where can I get a good steak?"

"Down the street in the Sawyer House. Best food in town."

"Better than here?"

The clerk looked around, then said, "Much better. But they don't do breakfast."

"And how's the breakfast here?"

"It's simple, but good."

"I'll try it tomorrow. Thanks."

He had to walk past the Sawyer House to get to the Dundee Hotel. The clerk there, an older man, was happy to let him look at the register.

"We have quite a few of the players registered here, sir."

"I can see that." Clint pushed the book back to the clerk. "Is Mr. Masterson in his room?"

"As far as I know," the clerk said. "He should be coming down for his supper, soon. He's eaten at the same time since he got here three days ago."

"Does he eat here?"

"No, sir," the clerk said. "The Sawyer House."

"Ah," Clint said, "then instead of bothering him in his room, I'll see him there."

"Yes, sir." The clerk looked around and then lowered his voice. "I won't tell him you were here looking for him."

"Thank you," Clint said, and left.

As he exited the Dundee, he saw the Opera House across the street. It was a square block of a building with a marque over the front door. He wondered if E.P. Milton had his eye on the place.

As he turned to walk away, he bumped right into a well-dressed woman.

"Oh!" she said. "I'm sorry, I wasn't looking where I was going."

"No, no," Clint said, "it was my fault. I was looking at the Opera House."

She was a tall, stately woman in her thirties, with a pretty face dominated by great big, blue eyes.

"Do you like opera?" she asked.

"I'm afraid I don't understand it," Clint said.

"Then if you're not here for opera, you must be here for poker."

"As a matter of fact, I am."

"Hopefully I'll see you across the table," she said, and continued on before he could even ask her name.

Clint had not played serious poker for some time and had only started again a few months ago. This would be his first high stakes game in several years, so he was sure there would be players—like this lady—he had never heard of. Bat Masterson could fill him in over a meal.

As he headed for the Sawyer House, the lady with the blue eyes was still on his mind . . .

***

The Sawyer House had a very large interior, and probably could have fit double the amount of tables, but they obviously wanted to have space to offer people privacy during their meal. When he walked in, he could see that several tables were still open, and one in particular appealed to him.

"That one," he told the dark-suited host, "back there."

"Of course, sir," the man said. "An excellent view of the entire room. Follow me, please."

He led Clint to the table, where he sat with his back to the wall. He'd be able to see Bat Masterson as soon as he entered.

"Enjoy your dinner, sir," the man said, and walked away.

Clint looked around, wondering how many other tables were occupied by poker players.

A waiter came over and asked, "Would you like a menu, sir?"

"I'll have a steak," he told the waiter, "with all the trimmings."

"Coffee or beer, sir?"

"Beer with the meal, coffee after."

"Yes, sir."

"I understand Bat Masterson takes his meals here."

"Oh, yes, sir," the waiter said. "He usually sits there." He indicated another back table.

"Well, when he comes in, maybe you can convince him to join me at this table."

"I'll try to do that, sir."

The waiter withdrew but returned quickly with a mug of beer.

Chapter Eleven

Bat showed up at the front door before Clint's steak came. The waiter intercepted him and spoke to him, at which time Bat looked over at Clint's table, and nodded. He walked over with a big smile on his face.

"Glad you made it," he said, sitting across from Clint. "I've been waiting here for three days."

"So I heard from the desk clerk," Clint said.

"The usual, Mr. Masterson?" the waiter asked.

"You bet, Carl."

"Comin' up, sir."

"The steak's good here," Bat said. "The best in town, anyway."

"I ordered it."

"What took you so long to get here?"

"I stopped in Blackhawk, got involved in the theater there."

"I heard about that," Bat said. "Miners are moving out, theater people are moving in. Doesn't sound like a good exchange, to me."

"Folks in Blackhawk don't like it much, either. And it looks like they're going to be coming here, next."

"They already have an opera house," Bat said. "Now a theater?"

"Where's the poker game happening," Clint asked.

"The saloon is called The Blue Rose," Bat said. "Sounds more like the title of an opera, to me. But it's got a big back room."

"How many players are there?" Clint asked.

"Ten tables, six players per table," Bat said.

"I looked at both hotel registers, and didn't recognize a lot of names."

"Some of the regulars ain't here, but these past couple of years that you've been out of it, some new ones have come along."

The waiter came with both their meals and set the plates down, then another approached with two beers.

"Enjoy, gents."

"The waiters hereabouts sound like they followed the theater people from the East," Clint said.

"The West ain't what it used to be," Bat said.

"Why's Luke not here?" Clint asked about their friend, Luke Short.

"He has other business," Bat said.

They cut into their steaks as they talked. Clint's yielded a lot of red, while Bat's was more well done.

"So who are the players to watch out for?" Clint asked.

"Well," Bat said, "there's me, and then you."

"Come on."

"I've always told you that you're a natural," Bat said. "I'm glad you're back in the game."

"What about a lovely lady with big, blue eyes."

Bat looked surprised.

"Where did you meet Lady Poker."

"Lady Poker?"

"That's what they've started calling her," Bat said. "Her name's Victoria Belmont."

"Well, I saw her on the street, across the street from the opera house."

"And you didn't get her name?" Bat asked. "You're slipping, Clint."

"Might be," Clint agreed. "I suppose I was kind of stunned by those eyes."

"Well, she uses those eyes when she plays, so you better hope you're not sitting right across the table from her. You'd be better off next to her, so you don't have to look into them the whole time."

"I'll remember that. Who else . . ."

***

Bat reeled off a few more names to beware of while they ate.

"Are all the players here?" Clint asked.

"Yep," Bat said, "you're the last one to arrive. Tomorrow morning we'll all have to check in at the Blue Rose and draw for our spots."

The waiter cleared their plates and brought coffee and pie for dessert. They didn't have peach, so Clint took apple. Bat had rhubarb, which Clint hated.

"Have you had any dealings with the local sheriff?" Clint asked.

"Just to meet 'im," Bat said. "Wood seems like an old-time lawman who's pretty tired out."

"Well, he tried to arrest me as soon as I got to town."

"What?" Bat asked. "What the hell for?"

"He said the law in Blackhawk asked him to 'detain' me."

"On what charge?"

"No charge."

"And?"

"I told him if he wanted to arrest me, he'd have to use force," Clint said.

"And he backed down."

"He just got real quiet, and I walked out of his office."

"I bet you won't be seein' him again," Bat said.

"Who's running this game?"

"The owner of the Blue Rose," Bat said. "His name's Wilford Tweedy."

"Really?" Clint asked. "Tweedy?"

"Don't make fun of his name," Bat said. "He doesn't like it."

"Hey, he's the man in charge," Clint said. "I'll respect him for that. Hopefully, he's got some authority in town and can keep the sheriff away from me."

"I'm pretty sure you accomplished that all by yourself."

Chapter Twelve

After they left the Sawyer Bat said, "Most of the players have been drinkin' at the Blue Rose in the evenings. There ain't much else to do here."

"No opera?" Clint asked.

"Not since I've been here. Come on, you can meet some of the other players."

"Like Lady Poker?"

"She seems to like her hotel room," Bat said. "She doesn't drink in the Blue Rose. Her room's down the hall from mine and I don't ever hear her going in or out. I'm surprised you ran into her on the street. Maybe she was shopping."

"She wasn't carrying anything," Clint said. "Far as I could see, she was just walking."

As they approached the Blue Rose, Clint saw two other men entering ahead of them. They were dressed in trail clothes, as he was, while Bat had his usual suit, vest and bowler hat ensemble. He was also carrying his silver-tipped cane.

When they entered, Clint was impressed by the spaciousness of the room. The bar seemed to run the entire length and had two bartenders behind it. There were all types of table games, as well as a wheel of fortune in the center of the room.

There were a few men strung out along the long bar. Otherwise, most of them were seated at tables, by twos, threes and fours.

Bat led Clint to the bar, where one of the bartenders came running over.

"Evenin', Mr. Masterson," he said. "Whataya have?"

"My friend and I will have a beer, Jerry," Bat said.

"Comin' up."

The bartender quickly drew the two beers and delivered them without spilling a drop.

"I notice nobody's coming over to say hello to you," Clint said.

"That's the way I like it," Bat said. "If I want to talk to anyone, I'll go over to them."

"Any of the players you warned me about in here now?"

"Over at that table in the corner, the fella with the yellow-and-red vest, that's Dwight Ketchem. He thinks he's a clothes horse. Always has a brightly colored vest on. Looks like a clown to me. All he needs is a big red nose."

"Who's that sitting with him?"

"Not one of the players," Bat said, "but he stays close to Ketchem."

"Watching his back?"

"Could be," Bat said. "Ketchem's attitude leaves him open for trouble." Bat looked around. "Over there, with the two girls talking to him. The young, handsome one is Johnny Dark. He looks young, but he's a patient card player. And, as you can see, the girls like him."

"Who's the other one?"

"That's big-and-beefy Bill Hagen. He'll probably be the first one out, since he never folds."

"Why's he even play?"

"Who knows? He's got the money."

"He doesn't dress like it."

"He spends his money on whiskey and poker. And, oh yeah, whores."

"Where's Mr. Tweedy?"

"He's not here, probably in his office. But he comes out late at night to make the rounds. And to make sure all his money makers are here."

"What's his cut?"

"A third," Bat said, "which is a lot considering the buy-in is ten thousand and there are sixty players."

Clint whistled. "A total pot six hundred thousand, with Tweedy taking two hundred of it."

"With four hundred thousand left," Bat said, doing the math, "the winner gets sixty percent, second gets twenty, third and fourth get ten."

"Forty thousand isn't bad for fourth," Clint said. "No wonder there's so much security."

Upon entering Clint became aware of the four men armed with shotguns, in each corner of the room.

"Oh yeah, Tweedy is determined that nothing goes wrong."

"It looks pretty safe in here."

"Plus, he's not collecting guns from the players," Bat said. "So the only thing that might go wrong is a shoot-out at a table."

Chapter Thirteen

Bat and Clint got another beer each and took them to a table.

"Tell me about Blackhawk," Bat said. "Maybe we can figure out why they wanted you arrested."

It didn't take long to relay to Bat his experience in Blackhawk.

"I can't imagine you did anything to those theater people to get yourself arrested," Bat said.

"Me neither," Clint said. "Even the sheriff here didn't have a reason."

"You may never find out."

"As long as nobody tries it again, I'm satisfied," Clint said.

Slowly, the saloon began to fill, with townspeople and poker players. Some of the players exchanged a nod with Bat, but none came over to the table.

There were two girls working the floor, one in a yellow dress, one in a red one. They spent most of their time talking with Johnny Dark, but the one in red finally came to their table.

"You gents want another drink?"

"Yes, thanks," Bat said. "Two beers."

"Comin' up."

She brought them two fresh beers, then went back to flirting with Johnny Dark.

As it got later, a man came down the stairs from the second floor.

"There's Tweedy," Bat said.

"Will he approach you, or is he afraid?"

"Nobody's afraid," Bat said, "they're just respectful. But yes, he will come over. I'll introduce you."

Tweedy stopped at several tables to exchange pleasantries before finally coming over to Bat's. He was tall, well-dressed, in his forties.

" 'evening, Bat," he said.

"Good evening, Wilford. I want you to meet a friend of mine, Clint Adams."

Clint stood and the two men shook hands.

"Glad to meet you, Mr. Tweedy."

"I'm very happy to meet you, Mr. Adams. I'm thrilled to have someone of your caliber in this contest. And you'll have to call me Wilford."

"And you can call me Clint. Join us for a drink?"

"I think I will. Thanks."

Tweedy sat and the girl in the yellow dress came running over. Both girls were pretty, in their twenties, this one a brunette, and the girl in red was a blonde.

"Drink, boss?" she asked.

"I'll have a beer, Mae. Thanks."

"You gents?"

"We're good for now, thanks," Bat said.

She hurried to the bar and back with Tweedy's beer.

"Thank you, Mae."

Mae rushed back to Johnny Dark's table, not wanting to leave him alone too long with the blonde.

"I hope you know I can't put you at the same table to start," Tweedy said.

"That's fine with us," Bat said. "The longer we can stay away from each other, the better."

"Good," Tweedy said, "because you'll have to earn your way to the same table."

"I expect we'll both be on that final table," Bat said.

"You have a lot of confidence, Bat," Tweedy said. "In both of you."

"Yes, well, Bat has to have it for both of us," Clint said.

"You don't think you're good enough, Clint?" Tweedy asked.

"I've been away awhile."

"Don't worry," Bat said. "He's good enough."

"Good," Tweedy said. "I'd hate to have one of my marquee names drop out too early."

He finished his beer and stood up.

"Enjoy your evening," he said. "I'll see you all in the morning."

"Good night, Wilford," Bat said.

"He's smooth," Clint said.

"Too smooth?" Bat asked.

"I don't know," Clint said. "There's a lot of money involved, here."

"You haven't handed yours over yet," Bat said. "You can back out. Especially since you might get arrested at any moment."

"I'm not worried about that," Clint said, "and I'm not going anywhere. You just want me to leave sheep for you to fleece."

"That's ridiculous," Bat said. "There's enough fleecing here for both of us. Of course, I'll finish first, and you'll finish second."

"Of course," Clint said, and they both laughed.

***

Clint quit the Blue Rose before Bat, and went to his hotel to turn in. He half expected to see the sheriff waiting in the lobby, maybe even with a deputy or two, but no one was there.

He stopped at the desk for a word with the clerk.

"Has anyone been in here looking for me, today?" he asked.

"No, sir."

"Not even the sheriff?"

"No, sir. In fact, I haven't seen the sheriff in days."

"Doesn't he make rounds?"

"He's supposed to, yes," the clerk said, "but he hardly does."

"I see. Okay." Clint started away, then stopped and turned back. "You said you haven't seen the sheriff in days?"

"Well," the clerk said, "not until he came here earlier, looking for you. And you left with him."

"And not since then?"

"Not since," the clerk said, "and not much before."

"Do you know if the sheriff has deputies?"

"Part timers," the clerk said. "Nobody full time."

"I see. Okay, thanks."

"Anytime, sir. My name's Tom, if I can be of any more help."

"Okay, Tom," Clint said, "I'll keep that in mind."

Clint went up to his room and got himself comfortable. He hung his gunbelt on the bed post, removed his boots, then reclined on the bed. He had a book in his saddlebags, a copy of Sir Walter Scott's *Ivanhoe,* which he hadn't yet finished, but he didn't take it out. He couldn't finish it before the poker game started, and then after he wouldn't have time. So, he simply clasped his hands behind his head, stared at the ceiling, and thought about what he would do with the money if he won the poker challenge, or even came in second, as Bat suggested.

Chapter Fourteen

In the morning, Clint decided to have breakfast in his hotel before walking over to the Blue Rose Saloon. He ordered a simple ham-and-eggs plate, and it was fine, accompanied by a basket of biscuits.

After breakfast he went over to the saloon to sign up for the poker challenge. He saw men going in as he approached, and, once inside, saw a couple of lines of men waiting to sign up.

"It looks like we're all here," a woman said, from behind him.

He turned and saw those blue eyes of the woman they called Lady Poker. She was wearing a tight-fitting grey suit.

"Well, hello," Clint said. "Yes, I guess we're all here, and it looks like you're the only lady."

"Good," she said, "I'll take that as an advantage. By the way, we didn't properly meet yesterday. My name is Veronica Belmont."

"I know," he said. "I've been told they call you Lady Poker."

"And they call you the Gunsmith. It's a pleasure to formally meet you."

They shook hands.

"How do you know who I am?" he asked.

"Somebody mentioned it to me. Shall we get in line?"

"After you," he said.

"Thanks."

They chose a line and stood in it. Clint noticed they were getting a lot of stares.

"You're getting a lot of attention," he said.

"That's very kind, but you don't think they're looking at you? You're pretty infamous, you know."

"I'm just here to play poker."

The line moved fairly quickly, and before long they had both signed up and handed over their buy-in.

The bar was open so Clint said, "Can I buy you a drink?"

"A little early, isn't it?" she asked.

"Coffee, then."

"Coffee'd be fine."

They each had the bartender bring them a coffee, then walked to an empty table. From there Clint could watch the other players sign in.

"Which table did you get?" Clint asked her.

"Table five. You?"

"Table eight."

"Too bad," she said. "I wanted to go up against you early."

"We'll see what happens."

Clint saw Bat enter, and, since the lines were much shorter, he signed in quickly. After getting his table number, he went to the bar for a cup of coffee, then carried it over.

"Mind if I join you?" he asked.

"Not at all, Mr. Masterson," Lady Poker said.

"Have a seat, Bat," Clint replied.

"What number did you get, Mr. Masterson?" she asked him.

He held his number up and said, "Table One. And call me Bat."

"All right, Bat," she said. "I suggest both you gents call me Veronica."

"Not Ronnie?" Bat asked.

She made a face and said, "Never!"

"Who else is at your table, Bat?"

"I don't know," Bat said. "I'll find out when we start playing."

"And when's that going to be?" Clint asked.

"We start at noon," Bat said. "Tweedy wants to make sure everybody gets a chance to sign up. Seems some of us can oversleep."

"And if that happens during the game?" Clint asked.

"Anyone who doesn't show up on time for the start gets kicked out," Bat said.

"Sounds fair," Veronica said.

"So we've got three hours to wait before we start," Clint said.

"What should we do til then?"

"What about some three handed?" Veronica asked. "We could use the back room."

"Would Tweedy object?" Clint asked Bat.

"No," Bat said. "In fact, there have been some games back there already."

"We'll need a deck of cards from the bartender," Clint said.

"No need," Bat said, taking a deck from his vest.

"Then let's go," Veronica said.

They stood up and walked to the back room, which Clint hadn't seen, yet. The doorway was curtained, and, when they walked through, Clint saw the ten empty poker tables.

"Everybody must be waiting til noon," Bat said.

"Shall we sit here?" Veronica asked, pointing to the first table.

"Too close to the door," Bat said.

"Back there, where we can see the whole room," Clint said.

They walked to the back and sat. Bat took the cards out, shuffled and dealt . . .

Chapter Fifteen

They played for a couple of hours with the money going back and forth, and by the time they quit, they were all even.

"I suppose it's good we're all starting at different tables," Veronica said. "Seems we're pretty evenly matched."

Clint agreed, even though he felt sure Bat was holding back, only playing to pass the time, not to win.

They stepped back out into the saloon's main room and saw that business had started for the day. Wilford Tweedy was standing at the bar with what looked like a glass of brandy.

"Ah, you three were back there, warming up, eh?" he asked, as they approached.

"Passing the time," Bat said.

"Well, we start in less than an hour," Tweedy said.

"Is the saloon going to be doing business as usual during the game?" Clint asked.

"Oh, yes," Tweedy said. "I can't really afford to shut down."

Clint looked around, didn't see the four security men, just one with a shotgun.

"What about security?" he asked.

"That'll be out in full force when we start," Tweedy said. "And I'll have two more men back there. If it's not too early for you folks, I'll buy you a drink."

"I'd like some of that brandy you're having," Veronica said.

"Of course. Bat?"

"Yes, I'll take some."

"Mr. Adams?"

"A beer will do me."

Tweedy waved down a bartender and put in the order.

"I'm sure you folks are wondering about meal breaks," he said. "Today we'll have sandwiches available in the back room. Tonight, there'll be a supper break. Starting tomorrow, there will be a lunch break and a supper break."

The bartender came with the drinks, and Tweedy handed them out.

"Here's to good luck," Tweedy said, raising his glass.

The others raised their glasses, as well.

Tweedy took out a pocket watch and looked at it.

"Half an hour," he said. "The players should begin to file in."

As he said that, the batwing doors opened, and men started to pour in.

"Gentlemen and Lady," Tweedy said, "it's time."

Chapter Sixteen

Competitors filed into the back room and took their assigned seats. The players at Clint's table all introduced themselves. None of them were the men Bat had warned him about.

There were no house dealers, so the deal would pass from player to player. That suited Clint just fine. You could tell a lot about a player from the way he handled the cards—the shuffle, and then the deal.

Within the first hour, two players busted out of the game from Clint's table, and a few from other tables, including big, beefy Bill Hagen. The players wouldn't be shuffled about until a table or two got down to three players. Once the first few players busted out, the rest seemed to be holding their own.

The two girls brought sandwiches in for a late lunch, and carried them from table to table. Clint didn't like to eat or drink while he played, so he passed. He noticed that Bat and Veronica did the same. But plenty of the others took a sandwich and wolfed it down between hands.

At seven, Wilford Tweedy appeared and announced, "We're taking a break for supper, people. Please be back here by eight-thirty. You're all welcome at the Sawyer House. Supper's not free, but you'll get a bargain price. Enjoy!"

The players stood and walked out of the room. The two girls began cleaning sandwich crumbs and cigarette ash from the tables, getting them ready for the next round of play.

Bat and Veronica came over to Clint's table as he got to his feet.

"Sawyers?" Bat asked.

"Where else?" Clint asked. "The food's good and we get a bargain price."

"You gents mind if I join you?" Veronica asked.

"We insist on it," Bat said.

They left the Blue Rose together and walked to Sawyers. Most of their suppers had been served from five-to-seven, so there were plenty of tables for the poker players, many of whom were already there.

Clint and Bat chose a table that suited them, in the back, from where they could both see the rest of the room. The trio studied the impressive menu and ordered, then talked about the first day of play.

"You were right about that Hagen fellow," Clint said. "He was the first one out, because he never folded, no matter what he had."

"Now that's somebody who plays just because he enjoys it," Veronica said. "Not to win."

"If you don't play to win, there's no point in playing," Bat said. "Pure and simple."

At that point, a ruckus erupted across the room. It looked like Johnny Dark had gotten into an argument with one of the other players. Dark was sitting with Bill Hagen, and a man was standing alongside the table, shaking his fist at Dark.

". . . if you keep it up, I'm gonna mess up that pretty face of yours so no girl will like it," the man was saying.

"Take it easy, Sam," Johnny Dark said. "I was just making a comment."

"And I didn't like it!" the man called Sam said. "In fact, I just might put a bullet between your eyes!"

As the man opened his fist and went for his gun, Big Bill Hagen moved with surprising speed. He came out of his chair, grabbed the man's hand and yanked it behind his back.

"Ow, Jesus, you're breakin' my arm!"

"Whataya want me to do with him, Johnny?" Hagen asked.

"Just walk him outside, Bill, and let him cool off."

Hagen turned the man around and walked him right out the door, then came back in. As he did, three more men stood up from their table.

"Ya shouldn'ta done that, Bill," one of them said. "Now we gotta teach ya."

Clint noticed that Hagen didn't wear a gun. Apparently, he felt he could handle any situation with his fists.

"You fellas better siddown," he said.

The three of them drew their guns and Hagen steeled himself.

"Hold it!" Clint shouted, standing up.

Everybody in the room looked at him.

"He doesn't have a gun," Clint said. "You boys better all drop yours to the floor."

"This ain't your business, Adams," one of the men said.

"You're interrupting my supper," Clint said, "that makes it my business. Now drop those guns."

The three men all looked at each other, and then dropped their guns.

"Now if you want to settle this, do it outside."

"That suits me," Hagen said.

He turned and stormed outside. The three men followed him. From the sound of it, the fight didn't last very long, and Hagen came back in.

"Thanks, Mr. Adams," he said, and sat back down with Johnny Dark.

Clint sat, as one of the waiters picked up the three guns and took them to the kitchen.

Chapter Seventeen

"I thought you were going to shoot those men," Veronica said.

"There was no reason," Clint said. "I knew I could get them to drop their guns."

"How did you know they wouldn't shoot you?" she asked.

"That's something you learn when you live by the gun," Bat said. "You can tell when a man will use it, and when he won't."

"And that big man beat them all up?"

"I'm sure he left them lying face down in the dirt," Clint said. "But they'll be back for their guns, eventually."

"What about the sheriff?"

"I met him," Clint said. "I doubt he'll do anything."

"Are those men in the game?" she asked. "Will they make trouble there?"

"The first man who was yelling at Johnny Dark, he's a player," Bat said. "The others are just his friends. If he makes trouble during the game, he'll be thrown out."

"I think he'll play himself out of the game soon," Clint said. "Young Johnny seems to have gotten under his skin."

"You think he uses his good looks that way?" Veronica asked.

"I'm sure he uses whatever he's got," Clint said. "As we all do."

"Like you use those eyes," Bat said.

"What?" she said. "I use my poker playing, and that's all."

"You can't help but use those eyes, Veronica," Bat said. "I'd like to see you and Johnny at the same table. Your eyes against his smile."

"His smile won't affect me at all," she said. "He's very young."

"He is that," Clint said, "but I agree. It would be interesting."

"I think when we end up at the same table," she said, "you'll both see my ability with the cards."

Clint looked at Bat and said, "Maybe we should root for someone else to bust her out of the game before that can happen."

"I believe the three of us will make up half the final table," Veronica said. "Then it'll get interesting."

"We've got a lot of other players to get past, first," Bat said. "Anything can happen."

"What about when we leave here?" she asked. "Those men might still be out there."

"If they are," Clint said, "they have no guns. I don't think anything will happen."

"Not today, anyway," Bat added.

"I hope not," Veronica said. "I think we better get back to the Blue Rose."

As they got up to leave, so did Johnny Dark and Billy Hagen.

Dark came up alongside Clint and said, "Thanks for what you did. They might've shot Billy down for defending me."

"I think you better get your friend to wear a gun," Bat said.

"He doesn't like guns," Johnny said. "He prefers using his bare hands."

"So did Bear River Tom Smith," Clint said, "and look what happened to him."

Tom Smith was a lawman in Abilene. He preferred not to use a gun and was soon killed. He was replaced by Wild Bill Hickok who, years later, was himself shot and killed in Deadwood, South Dakota.

"Billy will be fine," Johnny said. "I think he would've handled those three if you hadn't stepped in, but you have my thanks."

As Johnny Dark walked on ahead, Veronica asked Clint, "How would he have handled three armed men when he wasn't armed, himself?"

"I guess we'll never find out," Clint said.

***

Back in the Blue Rose they returned to their tables. The game went on until two a.m., when Wilford Tweedy came in and called a halt. Of the original sixty players, forty-one remained, including Clint, Bat, Veronica and Johnny Dark.

The saloon remained open until three, so Clint, Bat and Veronica went to the bar for a drink. Johnny Dark walked by with one of the saloon girls on each arm, and Bill Hagen trailing behind. He smiled at the three of them.

"I have a feeling Johnny's night is just getting started," Bat said.

"Well, mine's ending," Veronica said. "Clint, I'm at the Dundee. Would you walk me there? I'm worried those rowdy cowboys might still be on the street."

"Of course," Clint said, finishing his beer. "Goodnight, Bat."

"Good night, Bat," Veronica echoed.

Bat didn't bother pointing out to her that he was also at the Dundee.

"Good night to you both," he said, and ordered another beer.

Chapter Eighteen

Clint and Veronica walked to the Dundee hotel through the dark streets of Central City.

"Are you worried?" she asked him.

"About those three from earlier? Not really."

"No," she said, "I mean about me."

"Why should I worry about you?"

"About why I asked you to walk me to my hotel, when I know Bat is also staying there."

"I just thought you don't like Bat."

She laughed and said, "I like him just fine."

"My mistake."

"I think you're being funny," she said. "You know why I asked you to walk me."

"Let's say I have an idea," Clint said, "and I hope I'm right."

"Oh," she said, "I think you are."

When they got to the Dundee there were no more questions. Clint entered the hotel with Veronica and walked her all the way to her door.

He waited while she fit the key into the lock and then followed her in. Without a word, she turned and came into his arms. They stood that way with one kiss lasting a long time. When she stepped back, she was flushed and breathless. She proceeded to strip off her clothes until she stood naked in front of him. Her breasts were high and firm, her legs long and sleek, but even with every inch of her in view, he was drawn to her blue eyes.

"This isn't going to work if you stay dressed," she told him.

He smiled, unstrapped his gunbelt and walked past her to hang it on the bed post. Then she watched as he undressed, starting with his boots. By the time he was naked, his cock was hard, as a result of that long kiss and those blue eyes.

She came to him, and they pressed their naked bodies together as they shared another long kiss. Her nipples became so hard they felt like small stones against his chest.

She stepped back from him and took a moment to draw the blanket and sheets down on the bed. Then she turned and reached for his cock, cradling it in both hands, stroking it as she sat on the bed. From that position she was able to bend and take him into her mouth.

She cradled his testicles in her hands as she sucked him, bobbing her head up and down, as he ran his hands over her smooth flesh, tracing the beautiful line of her back up and down.

When she finally released him from her mouth, she settled down onto her back, opening her long legs for him. He could have mounted her there and then and driven his cock into her, but the fragrance of her wetness drew his attention, and he suddenly wanted nothing more than to taste her.

He knelt between her widespread legs and pressed his face to her pussy. She was already so wet that he went right in with his tongue and began to lick her. She reached down to grab his head and hold him there, as if he had any intention of moving away. He continued to lick until she began to writhe beneath him, closing her thighs around his head and moaning out loud.

As much as he licked her, she continued to gush her sweet juices all over his face.

"Oh, please, please," she said, grabbing for him, "put it in me now."

Never one to make a lady beg, he crawled up on her and drove his hard cock right into her steamy depth, where she gripped him wetly . . .

***

"I told you we shoulda taken him in the street," Dave Griff said.

"Not while he was with that woman," Lonnie George said. "We just want him. She didn't do nothin' to us."

"Lonnie's right," Pete Sheen said. "It's just him we want. We'll wait for him to come out."

"Too bad it's so dark," Dave said. "I wanna see his face when we fill him fulla lead."

"You're an idiot," Lonnie said. "We're doin' this *because* it's dark. We don't want nobody to see us."

"We're killin' the Gunsmith," Griff said. "This could make us famous."

"I don't wanna be famous," Sheen said. "I just wanna pay him back for shamin' us in that restaurant."

"That's just what we're gonna do," Lonnie said, "pay him back."

"It's a good thing Bat Masterson ain't with him," Griff said.

"We got nothin' against Masterson," Sheen said. "It's just the damn Gunsmith."

"Soon to be the dead Gunsmith," Sheen said, and they all laughed.

Chapter Nineteen

Clint and Veronica rested, made love, and rested again.

"Why don't you stay the night?" she asked.

"If I'm going to play poker tomorrow, I'll need to get some rest."

"I suppose you're right," she said, "but this was fun."

"A lot of fun," he agreed.

She watched as he stood up and got dressed.

"You have to take that with you wherever you go, don't you?" she asked, as he strapped on his gun.

"Yes," he said, "it's become part of me, out of necessity."

"And yet you didn't use it when you could have on those men," she said.

"I only use it when I absolutely have to," he told her.

"You're an amazing man."

"I just try to do the right thing."

"Well," she said, "you certainly did that with me."

He leaned over and kissed her.

"Good night, Veronica.

"Good night, Clint."

He went to the door and opened it, but before he could leave, she said, "You know this doesn't mean I won't try to beat you if we end up on the same table."

"Exactly how I feel," he said, and left.

***

"He's been in there a long time," Sheen said.

"He's gettin' his wick wet," Griff said. "That just means he's gonna be easier to take."

"Why?" Sheen asked.

"Whataya think, dummy?" Lonnie said. "He's gonna be worn out."

"Well, if he doesn't come out soon, I'm gonna be worn out," Griff said.

"He'll be out soon," Lonnie said, "You better get across the street. And don't start shootin' until I do."

"Right," Griff said, and ran across.

"He better not mess this up," Sheen said.

"If he fires first, we'll just leave him to it," Lonnie said. "We can always get Adams another time."

"Wait," Sheen said, "there he is, in the lobby."

"Okay," Lonnie said, "move down the street and get set."

They couldn't signal Griff across the street, but they hoped he saw Adams in the lobby, too.

***

When Clint stepped out of the hotel, he felt there was something in the air. He could never explain it, but it was an instinct. When someone was laying for him, he knew it.

He stepped into the street, ready for anything.

They weren't pros, because they didn't fire at the same time. The first shots missed, and by the time the others joined in, Clint was on the move.

He dove to the right, found cover behind a horse trough. Lead began to punch into the other side of it, and water spilled out.

The street was dark. Central City had not yet installed lights. The shooters were using the dark, but Clint could do the same. Where he was now, there was some light from the hotel.

He moved to the other end of the trough, then rolled out into the open, away from the hotel lights, into the dark.

"Where is he?" somebody shouted, and it was enough to tell Clint where the man was. Keeping low, he ran that way.

"Shut up!" somebody else called.

Luckily, there was very little moonlight. Clint moved in the direction of the first voice.

"Move!" somebody shouted, and Clint assumed that was an order for all the shooters.

He stood up as a man broke from cover and started to run. He fired once. The man stumbled, caught his balance, but then fell.

Satisfied that he'd gotten one, he turned and looked across the street. Sure enough, two more had broken from cover to run, but they were going in opposite directions. He could only choose one and he did so quickly.

As Clint took off after the man, Bat Masterson came out of the hotel in shirt sleeves, gun in hand. Clint spotted him.

"The other way, Bat!" he called.

"Right."

Bat ran in the opposite direction. The streets were empty, and Clint could hear the man's footsteps ahead of him. He increased his speed until he spotted the shadow ahead of him.

"Hold it!" he said, and fired to either side of the shadow, spitting up dirt from the street.

"All right, all right!" the man shouted. He stopped and raised his hands. "Don't shoot."

Clint stopped about three feet from him.

"Turn around."

As he did, Clint recognized him as one of the men from the restaurant.

"What's your name?"

"Sheen."

"Okay, Mr. Sheen," Clint said, "you and me are going to the sheriff's office. As soon as you drop your gun."

The man was scared, that was obvious. The question was, was he scared enough to do something stupid?

"You can take the gun out of your holster with two fingers and drop it," Clint said, "or you can go for it." Clint holstered his own gun. "It's your choice."

"N-no," the man said, "no way." He lifted the gun from his holster with two fingers and dropped it to the ground.

"Good choice," Clint said, "Let's go."

He walked the man back toward the hotel, and stopped when they reached the body of the first man.

"What's his name?"

"It was Griff."

"And the other man?"

"W-what other man?"

"Oh, that's not a smart answer, Sheen. The man shouting the orders. The one who ran off and left you."

"Oh," Sheen said, "t-that was Lonnie George."

"Good man," Clint said. "Just keep making smart decisions, Sheen. Now let's go, the sheriff is waiting."

Chapter Twenty

On the way to the sheriff's office they ran into Bat, coming back.

"He got away," Bat said.

"That's okay," Clint said. "We've got a name, Lonnie George."

"Were they the same three as in the restaurant?" Bat asked.

"Yes, this one's name is Sheen. I left one lying in the street back there. I'm taking this one to the sheriff's office."

"You think the sheriff's going to be any help?"

"He can at least put this one in a cell," Clint said.

"Let's go, then," Bat said. "If you think the sheriff'll be there at this time of night."

"With shooting in the streets? He better be, if he wants to keep his job."

When they got to the sheriff's office, there was a light inside. Clint opened the door and pushed Sheen in ahead of him.

"I knew it had to be you," Sheriff Wood said. "What's goin' on?"

"This one and two of his friends tried to bushwhack me. One's in the street, dead, the other one ran away."

"What's your name?" the sheriff asked.

"Sheen."

"Put him in a cell," Clint said. "We've got the other one's name. Lonnie George."

"I know him," Wood said. He grabbed Sheen's arm. "Come on."

He pushed him into the cell block and Clint heard the clang of a cell door. Then Wood came back.

"What are you gonna do now?" he asked.

"I'm going to my hotel to get some sleep," Clint said. "Tomorrow I'm playing poker. It's your job to find this man, George."

"I'll find 'im," Wood said. "And I'll put him in a cell next to his friend."

"You also have a body to clean up off the street," Clint said.

"I'll get that done."

"This is your chance to be a real lawman, Wood," Clint said.

"I *am* a real lawman, damn you!" Wood shouted. "I've been at this job a long time."

"Good," Clint said, "then I'll depend on you to make sure George doesn't try for me again."

"He's no pro," Wood said. "Him and his friends hang around, do odd jobs, hire out their guns when they can, but they're no pros."

"That was obvious," Clint said. "If they were pros, I'd probably be dead."

"I don't want you dead, Adams," Sheriff Wood said, "not in my town."

"Good," Bat said, "we'll all make sure he doesn't get dead. Because if he does, I'm not going to be happy with you, Sheriff."

"Now, Mr. Masterson—"

"Forget it, Bat," Clint said. "The sheriff's going to do his job."

"Right," Wood said.

"I'll be in the Blue Rose tomorrow, playing poker," Clint said, "if you have some news for me."

"Right, right."

"Come on, Bat."

They went out the door and stopped just outside.

"You really going back to your hotel?" Bat asked.

"Not much else I can do this time of night," Clint said.

"Well, do me a favor and don't get yourself shot—you know what? Never mind. Come on, I'll walk you back."

"Bat—"

"Don't argue with me."

"All right," Clint said, "all right."

They started walking.

Chapter Twenty-One

The next morning Clint had a quick breakfast in his hotel, then went to the Blue Rose to start playing at nine a.m. He exchanged a good-morning nod with Bat, but neither spoke of what had happened the night before. With Veronica it was a different story.

When she saw Clint enter, she rushed to him and asked, "Oh my God, what was all the shooting last night?"

"Those three from the restaurant tried to bushwhack me," he said.

"What happened?"

He smiled.

"It didn't get done."

"Did you kill them?"

"I killed one, gave one to the sheriff, and the other one got away. But we have his name. I'm leaving it to the sheriff to find him."

"Do you think he will?"

"Well," Clint said, "he said he knew him, so I'd say yes—if he really wants to."

"But he's the law," she said. "He's got to."

"We'll see. Meanwhile, we better concentrate on poker."

"Yes, of course."

They were playing for about an hour when Wilford Tweedy came over to his table.

"Can we talk?"

"Sure."

He got up and followed Tweedy to the bar, where the saloon owner asked, "Drink?"

"Coffee."

Tweedy held two fingers up to the bartender, who brought two mugs of coffee, one of them topped off with some brandy.

"I heard what happened last night. I'm glad to see you're all right."

"They were sloppy," Clint said.

"But I'm concerned about something like that happening again, in here."

"I don't think anyone here is thinking about anything but poker."

"I just want you to know I have my security men on duty," Tweedy said. "If someone comes in looking for you, they're going to find trouble before they reach the back room. So you can just concentrate on your game."

"Good to hear."

Clint left the bar and went back to his game.

"Trouble?" one man asked him.

"No," Clint said, "everything is fine. Deal."

The games were all draw poker, five card stud or seven card stud. Clint's preference was draw. The choice of games around the six-player table were equal—two preferred draw, two five card stud, and two seven card. Over the course of the first three hours of the day several players busted out of their game. On Clint's table, after three hours, one player busted out. Most of the chips were sitting in front of Clint and a player named Mattingly. The others had their chip stacks dwindling.

After five hours Tweedy came in again and walked to Clint's table.

"The sheriff's at the bar, asking for you." He looked at the others. "You gents will have to excuse Mr. Adams for ten minutes." He looked at Clint. "No longer."

"No longer," Clint said.

He stood up, walked into the saloon and went to the bar, where Sheriff Wood was waiting.

"I've got ten minutes," he said. "What've you got?"

"Nothin'," Wood said. "So far I haven't been able to locate Lonnie George."

"He was running the last time I saw him," Clint said. "He might still be running. Have you questioned Sheen?"

"Yeah," Wood said. "He said they met in a small saloon on the edge of town called The Three Ladies. I went there, but nobody's seen 'im."

"I have to get back," Clint said. "Keep looking."

Clint walked back into the poker room, but instead of going to his table he went to Bat's.

"Lunch?" he asked.

Each player was allowed a half hour for lunch, an hour for supper.

"Why not? Gents, back in half-an-hour."

Bat stood and left his mountain of chips. There were two spotters in the room, to time the lunch and dinner breaks, and watch the chips.

Clint went to his table and said, "Lunch, gents. Be back in half-an-hour."

The players had the option of having sandwiches in the bar or finding their own outside. Since half-an-hour was hardly time enough to leave the saloon for lunch, Clint and Bat went to the bar and waved at one of the bartenders for sandwiches.

"You've got quite a mountain of chips in front of you," Clint said.

"There's not a decent player at the table," Bat said. "I should have them cleaned out by midnight."

"They'll rearrange the tables before then," Clint said. They had already rearranged the tables once, when they got down to thirty-six players. That made six tables of six players, but they were getting down to thirty, at which time they'd rearrange them again.

"Good," Bat said, "maybe there'll be some competition."

"What did Tweedy want?" Bat asked. "He pulled you out twice."

Clint told Bat what Tweedy said about security being alert for trouble, and then what the sheriff had to say.

"You think this lawman's on the up-and-up?" Bat asked.

"I haven't decided, yet."

They each finished one sandwich and washed it down with a beer.

"How are you boys doing?" Tweedy asked, joining them.

"I need some competition," Bat said. "I'm getting bored."

"You'd think you'd be happy just winning," Tweedy said.

"You'd think so, but no," Bat said. "I went to work for my money. So far it's been too easy."

"And you, Clint?"

"I'm not as good as Bat," Clint said. "I've had to work for my chips. I've got a fella named Mattingly at my table, who seems to know what he's doing."

"Mattingly's good," Bat said.

"Well, we should be resetting the tables soon," Tweedy said. "Maybe then you'll have your competition. Maybe even each other."

"We better get back," Clint said, and they returned to their games.

Chapter Twenty-Two

Two hours later the field of players got down to thirty. Tweedy came in and announced the tables would be reset. The players stood, one table was removed, and then he placed players, table-by-table. Bat and Clint both were seated with five different players. Clint didn't have to deal with Mattingly anymore, and Bat got a new group and would see if he had any competition now. Clint noticed Veronica was placed at a table with Johnny Dark. Clint thought that should prove interesting.

The two saloon girls would come in every so often and take drink orders. Clint could see they weren't pleased with Johnny Dark paying attention to Veronica's blue eyes.

"Drinks?" one asked the players at Clint's table.

They all took a drink but Clint. Two of them beers, three whiskies. Clint didn't mind when his opponents drank during play. It tended to make his job easier.

"Don't your mouth get dry durin' a game, Adams?" one man asked.

Clint grinned and said, "Losing makes me dry, so no."

The thirty players left proved to be very well matched. Only two more busted out by the time the supper break came around at seven.

Clint, Bat and Veronica all met at the bar, and went to the Sawyer House for supper. Many of the other players were there as well.

"If there's going to be more trouble, it'll probably happen here," Bat said, as they seated themselves.

"Veronica, maybe you should sit somewhere else."

"With who? Johnny Dark? He invited me to dine with him, you know."

"Why not take him up on it?" Clint asked.

"He's too young and full of himself," she said. "I prefer my men older, more seasoned."

"First time I've ever been called 'seasoned,' " Bat said, laughing.

Over their meals they talked about the players at each of their tables.

"I've got a little more talent at my table, now," Bat said.

"Johnny Dark is a better player than I thought he would be," Veronica said. "Between us, we have most of the chips."

"I've got nobody like Mattingly at my table, this time," Clint said. "My chip stacks are getting bigger."

"Like I expected," Bat said, "you and me are going to be at the final table."

"Well, make room for me," Veronica said. "I think Johnny Dark's going to be there too."

"And maybe Mattingly," Clint added.

"Got a couple of players at my table who might round out the sixth spot," Bat said.

While they talked, both Clint and Bat scanned the room for possible trouble. The other players there seemed intent on discussing their tables as well.

"I think Tweedy expected this thing to go longer," Bat said, "but I'm betting we get down to a final table tomorrow."

"What does he care how long it takes?" Veronica asked. "He gets his cut."

"I think he's picking up some business at the bar as well," Bat said.

"That's chicken feed compared to what he's making from this event," Clint said.

"This is his first year," Bat said. "I'm pretty sure he wants to make this an annual thing. He's hoping to pick up some more big names."

"Maybe he'll pick up Brady Hawkes next year," Clint said.

"And Bret and Bart," Bat said. "And for this money, Luke Short and Wyatt might sit in."

"Wyatt Earp?" Veronica said. "Do you know him?"

"We're all good friends," Bat said.

"Mainly because we know one of us isn't going to try to shoot the other," Clint said.

"Well," she said, "if this event's going to get more exciting, I might come back."

"I think we better concentrate on this event, right now," Clint said.

They turned their attention to their meals. Clint and Bat finished their steaks, and Veronica left her roast chicken picked clean.

Chapter Twenty-Three

They walked back to the Blue Rose, keeping their eyes open for trouble. When they reached the saloon and entered, both Bat and Clint breathed a sigh of relief.

"We've got ten minutes," Bat said. "Let's get a drink."

They went to the bar, ordered two beers and a brandy for Veronica. A quick look around the room showed many of the players sitting, waiting. Johnny Dark was at a table alone, but with the two saloon girls hanging on him. Mattingly was sitting with a couple of other players.

"The next five hours should tell the tale," Bat said.

"I don't think we're going to get rid of twenty-four more players in that time," Clint said.

"So maybe I'm a little too ambitious," Bat said. "I don't mind if we get to a final table tomorrow."

"That would suit me, as well," Veronica said. "I'll consider myself a winner to sit at a table with Bat Masterson." She looked at Clint. "No offense."

"None taken," Clint said. "Bat's the best."

She smiled and said, "We will see about that, won't we?"

"Yes, we will," Clint said.

Players began to stand and file into the back room.

"Time to go," Bat said.

"Let's wait til they're all seated," Clint said. "Finish our drinks."

They watched as the other players all went into the back room, and when their glasses were empty, they followed. Everyone was seated as they made their way to their tables.

"Now it gets interesting," one of the men said, and started dealing . . .

***

By the end of the night Clint's prediction turned out to be right. They weren't down to a final table. In fact, there were still twenty-four players, so the next morning when they showed up there would be four new table set-ups.

While all the players filed out, Clint, Bat and Veronica took a table in the saloon and had a drink.

"Bat," Clint said, "I'm thinking you should walk Veronica back to your hotel tonight, just in case."

"You think someone's going to try to kill you again?" Veronica asked.

"I don't know, but there's no point in taking chances. I don't want you catching a bullet meant for me."

Veronica looked disappointed that Clint wouldn't be coming back to her hotel with her, but she understood his concern.

When they left the saloon, Bat and Veronica walked off toward their hotel, and Clint decided to stop at the sheriff's office.

"How's your prisoner doing?" he asked, as he walked in.

"He's being quiet," Sheriff Wood said.

"No word on the whereabouts of Lonnie George?"

"None," Wood said, "I spoke to some men who know him, but they ain't seen him."

"Maybe he left town," Clint said.

"That's what I was thinkin'."

"You think he'd come back with more help?" Clint asked.

"Depends on just how humiliated you made him feel," the sheriff said.

"Enough to makc him try to kill me," Clint said.

"Then if I was you, I'd keep watchin' my back," the lawman said.

"That's just what I've been thinking," Clint said.

"There's a stage comin' in tomorrow evenin'," Wood said.

"Why tell me that?"

Wood shrugged.

"Just so you know."

"Good night, Sheriff."

" 'night, Mr. Adams."

Clint left the sheriff's office and headed back to his hotel, keeping very aware of his surroundings.

***

As it turned out, E.P. Milton had lied to Kit about leaving for Central City the next day. There was no stage that day. He wasn't able to leave for a couple of days, but eventually he was on his way. The stage made one stop halfway, at a stage stop, where he and the other passengers were fed and put up for the night.

By the time the stage left the next morning, he had a plan in mind for Clint Adams, and he hoped to put it into effect as soon as he arrived.

***

Clint was half hoping Veronica would show up at his hotel that night, but when she didn't, he was glad she hadn't walked there in the dark alone. Who knew if Lonnie George was still around, and if he might use Veronica to get back at him? They had both enjoyed themselves—and each other—in bed the night before, but this was better for her safety.

Whether it was another day or two before the poker game was over, when it was done, he was going to go looking for George himself. Just to put this whole thing to rest.

Chapter Twenty-Four

Clint was surprised to see Veronica in the lobby when he came down the next morning.

"Mind if I join you for breakfast?" she asked.

"Not at all."

They sat at a table together in the small hotel dining room.

"I missed you last night," she said, after they ordered.

"I thought about you, too," he said. "I half expected you to knock on my door."

"I thought about it," she said, "but decided not to walk in the dark by myself."

"I'm glad you didn't. I want you to stay safe."

"That's very sweet."

"Not so much," he said. "If you got killed, I'd feel guilty. I don't like feeling guilty."

"Still sweet," she said, as the waiter set down their food.

***

They walked to the Blue Rose together, Clint saw Tweedy at the bar, and they joined him there, while players entered the back room.

" 'morning," Clint said.

"Good morning to you both," Tweedy said. "The new tables are set up, Mr. Adams is at four, Lady Poker is at two."

"Where's Bat?"

"Three," Tweedy said. "I've kept you apart as long as I could. Sometime today that will probably end."

"Where are Dark and Mattingly?" Clint asked.

"Dark's at two, Mattingly's at five. This is going to become very interesting today."

"Good," Clint said.

At that moment Bat entered and joined them. They told him the table setups for the day.

"Let's get to it, then," Bat said. "I'm guessing I'll see you both at the final table."

"That's what I expected," Tweedy said. "I've kept you all apart, but I knew you'd end up together."

"We're playing poker," Clint said, "but it sounds like you're playing chess."

"Well put, Mr. Adams," Tweedy said, "very well put."

Clint, Bat and Veronica walked toward the back room.

"So I'm the queen?" she asked Clint.

He laughed and said, "Who else would it be?"

***

By the lunch break each table was down to four play-ers, for a total of twenty. They would remain at these tables until there were eighteen players, at which time one table would be eliminated, and there would be three. This didn't happen until the supper break. When they came back from Sawyers, they sat at the three tables, with Clint, Bat and Veronica each at separate ones. Dark was at Veronica's, and Mattingly at Clint's again.

***

When the poker game started after supper, the stage pulled in and stopped in front of the Dundee hotel. The sheriff was there for two reasons: to see if Lonnie George would get off, and to meet E.P. Milton.

"Mr. Milton," he said, as the theater director disem-barked.

"Sheriff Wood?" Milton said. "Is Clint Adams in your jail?"

"He's not."

"Why not?" Milton asked. "I thought you were asked to detain him?"

"He wouldn't let me."

"I beg your pardon?" Milton said. "I thought you were the law."

"I am," Wood said, "but he's the Gunsmith."

Milton accepted his bag as they passed it down from atop the coach.

"I see we're in front of a hotel," Milton said, looking up at it. "Is Mr. Adams staying here?"

"No," Wood said, "he's at the other hotel in town."

"Good," Milton said. "I'll stay here then. Where's Mr. Adams now?"

"He's at the Blue Rose Saloon, playing poker."

"Ah yes," Milton said, "I knew he was coming here for that. Is it still going on?"

"It is."

"Would I be able to interrupt?"

"I wouldn't advise it."

"I see," Milton said. "Where can I get a good meal?"

"The Sawyer House," Wood said.

"After that I'd like to see the opera house."

"I can show that to you," Wood said, "but it'll be dark by then. You might prefer to see it in the mornin'."

"Excellent," Milton said. "Shall we meet here at nine a.m.?"

"I can do that," the sheriff said.

Milton stepped up onto the boardwalk to enter the hotel, then asked the sheriff, "Are there bathing facilities here?"

"Yes, there are."

"Excellent," the man said, and went inside.

The sheriff turned as the driver dropped down from his perch.

"He's one of them theater people," he said to the lawman.

"Yeah, he is."

"Why's he think everythin' is 'excellent?' "

"You got me, Charlie."

Chapter Twenty-Five

Sheriff Wood went back to his office. He didn't like E.P. Milton, but he was aware of how much authority the man had accumulated since arriving in Blackhawk. The same thing might happen in Central City, so he decided to try and stay on the man's good side.

He stopped at a café to pick up some breakfast for the prisoner, Sheen. He didn't know how long he was going to be holding the man in a cell, so he wanted to keep him fed and alive.

***

When the game ended that night, they were down to thirteen players. The next day they would be down to two tables, one with six and one with seven players.

"We're almost there," Bat said, as they sat at a table in the saloon with drinks. "Tomorrow we'll get down to a final table. Three men at my table are almost busted."

"Same at mine," Veronica said. "Johnny and I will bust them all out by noon."

"Clint?"

"Mattingly and I should get the others out by noon."

"Then by lunch we should have a final table."

"And when two players bust out," Bat said, "we'll all be in the money."

"One of us is going to walk away with a lot of money," Bat said.

They all raised their glasses.

"May the best man—or woman—win," Clint said, and they clinked.

***

Bat walked Veronica back to the Dundee. Clint went to the sheriff's office.

"Who came in on the stage?" he asked.

"A few people," Wood said. "No sign of Lonnie George."

"Anybody you know?"

"I didn't know 'im until today, but I heard of 'im," Wood said. "Some theater guy named Milton. He's built himself a big name in Blackhawk."

"I know," Clint said. "I met him."

"You get on his wrong side?"

"Maybe," Clint said, "why?"

"He's the one who wanted me to detain you in a cell," Wood said.

"You don't say," Clint commented. "Where is he?"

"Stayin' at the Dundee," Wood said. "He wants me to show him the opera house tomorrow."

"Did he ask about me?"

"Yeah," Wood said. "I told 'im you was in the poker game. I told 'im it wouldn't be smart to interrupt you."

"So he'll wait until the game's over," Clint said.

"I expect so."

"Good," Clint said, "I can worry about him later. Did he have anybody with him? A girl, or another man?"

"There was a girl and two other men on the stage," Woods said, "but they didn't act like they was together."

"How's Sheen doing?"

"I'm keepin' him fed," Wood said, "and he's keepin' pretty quiet."

"Good," Clint said. "I guess depending on how close he and George were, he may come back for him. But I doubt it. Last I saw him, he was running hard, leaving his two friends behind."

"From what I know of Lonnie George, there's no loyalty in his heart."

"When are you taking Milton to the opera house?"

"Tomorrow mornin'. I'm meetin' him in front of his hotel at nine."

"Suits me that I won't run into him at my hotel," Clint said.

"I don't think he'll bother you until after your poker game," Wood said.

"We should be wrapping it up sometime tomorrow, I think," Clint said. "Then we'll find out what he wants and why he's here."

"When he sees how much smaller we are than Black-hawk," Wood said, "maybe he'll just turn around and go back."

"For Central City's sake, I hope so," Clint said. "You don't need theater people here."

"I agree."

"I'll check in with you sometime tomorrow, Sheriff," Clint said. "Good night."

" 'night, Mr. Adams."

Clint left the sheriff's office, wondering if he had been wrong about the man.

Chapter Twenty-Six

The next morning, E.P. Milton looked out his hotel window at the front street. The town was waking up, but there still wasn't much in the way of traffic. He would probably have abandoned his plan for a theater in Central City once he saw the town, but he still had his plan concerning the Gunsmith. He certainly would not get much of Clint Adams' attention until the poker game was finished, so until then he intended to take a look at the opera house and walk around town looking for a likely location.

He put on his suit jacket, checked his appearance in the mirror, and went downstairs to meet the sheriff.

***

Bat and Veronica joined Clint for breakfast in his hotel's small dining room. Once they had placed their orders, he told them who had come in on the stage the day before.

"Theater people here?" Bat asked. "They've hardly got enough people to keep their opera house going."

"I don't know what's on his mind," Clint said. "And I can't figure out why he sent a telegram to the sheriff, telling him to detain me."

"Is he a big man around here?" Veronica asked.

"He is in Blackhawk," Clint said. "Central City might be his next target."

"I don't see it," Bat said.

"Well," Clint said, "maybe Tweedy's Blue Rose will start bringing more people to town after this poker game."

"I can see Mr. Tweedy becoming a big man around here," Veronica said, "but not this theater gent."

"If I was Milton," Bat said, "I'd try to join forces with Tweedy."

"Maybe that's on his mind," Clint said.

"Well," Bat said, "there's no point in worrying about anything other than the game. One of us is walking away with two hundred and forty thousand dollars."

"What will you do if it's you, Bat?" Veronica asked.

"I've been wanting to open a big gambling house in San Francisco," he answered. "This money would certainly finance that venture."

"What about you, Clint?" she asked.

"I haven't really given it much thought," Clint said. "I suppose I'll put it in the bank, for now. What about you?"

"I've always wanted to see Europe," she said. "I'll be able to do that with a win, or with the eighty thousand dollars second prize."

Bat checked his watch and said, "We better get to it. If they start without us, none of us will get the money."

They left the hotel and walked to the Blue Rose. Inside, they saw the other players all sitting at tables. Johnny Dark was sitting alone, with the two saloon girls.

"Looks like he's got more going for him than his looks and charm," Bat said.

"He's actually pretty good," Veronica said.

"His charm and looks don't do anything for you?" Bat asked.

"Like I said before," Veronica said, "I like my men more seasoned."

Tweedy came down from his office and announced the start of the game. All the players rose and walked to the back room. Two tables had been set up in the center of the big room.

Bat and Veronica were at the same table with Johnny Dark. Clint was sitting with Mattingly and four other players he didn't think much of.

They each got a card, and the high card—Mattingly with a King—dealt the first hand . . .

***

E.P. Milton came out of the Dundee and saw Sheriff Woods waiting for him.

"Sheriff, good morning," he said. "Why don't I buy you breakfast, and then we can go to the opera house."

"Suits me, Mr. Milton."

"Where's a good place?"

"The Sawyer House is the best."

"Then lead the way," Milton said.

Wood took Milton to the Sawyer House, which seemed to impress the theater man. The sheriff was thinking maybe he should have taken Milton to a less impressive place.

Milton was further impressed when he saw that he could get an omelet. When it came and he tasted it, his eyebrows went up.

"This is very good," he told the sheriff, who had settled for a simple breakfast of bacon-and-eggs.

"Mr. Milton," Wood said, "what really brings you to Central City? It can't just be the opera house. Maybe it's just Clint Adams?"

If Milton was more interested in the Gunsmith than he was the town, that would suit Sheriff Wood just fine.

"I'm quite interested in the opera house," Milton said, "but you're right, I have other reasons, including the Gunsmith. But I think I'll take them one at a time, starting with the opera house. Although," he said, cutting into his omelet, "this breakfast is also a good start."

Chapter Twenty-Seven

Within the first hour Clint and Mattingly had disposed of two players, bringing their table down to four. Bat and Veronica's table had started with seven players and was now down to six, including Johnny Dark. Play remained that way until lunch.

Clint and Bat took a break together, stood at the bar with sandwiches.

"We're still at four," Clint said. "Most of the chips are sitting in front of me and Mattingly. The other two players are just hanging on."

"We started with seven, and we're still at five," Bat said. "It's obvious that Veronica, Johnny and I will take the other two out, but like you say, they're hanging on."

"When we get down to a final table, this game could go on for a while," Clint said. "Some of us seem evenly matched. Of course, you're the top man, so you'll have a target on your back."

"I realize that," Bat said, "but I'm counting on you to take some of the heat off me."

"I'll do what I can," Clint said.

"At least I'll know you're not conspiring with any one against me," Bat said.

"If anyone beats you, Bat, I want it to be me," Clint told his friend.

"Same here," Bat said, "but you're not going to beat me, Clint. Nobody is. Not for that pot. I've already got my location picked out for my casino hotel in San Francisco."

"I'll be there for the grand opening."

There'll be a free suite waiting for you, my friend."

They finished their sandwiches and went back to their tables . . .

***

After breakfast Sheriff Wood took Milton over to the opera house. Milton was less impressed than he had been with the Sawyer House.

"Doesn't look like much from the outside, does it?" he commented. "It just looks like a box."

Woods had the key, so he opened the front doors and they entered. The inside was dominated by red-and-gold brocade.

"This is better," Milton said, "but still not great. How often do you have someone here?"

"Not often enough," Wood said.

Milton ran his finger over a surface and came away with dust.

"I can see that."

***

At the supper break Clint, Bat and Veronica went to the Sawyer House.

"Okay, we're there," Bat said. "The final table is set."

The last six players were Clint, Bat, Veronica, Johnny Dark, Mattingly, and a man named Kenyon, who none of them knew.

"No more breaks from here on in," Bat said. "We play through until somebody wins."

"This could go on for some time," Veronica observed.

"That's the point," Clint said. "To not only see who the best player is, but who can stay awake and alert the whole time."

"A heavy meal tends to keep me awake," Bat said.

"That has the opposite effect on most men," Veronica said.

When they were shown to their table, Clint and Bat ordered the largest steak they could get. Veronica ordered an entire roast chicken.

While they waited for their food, Clint saw E.P. Milton enter the restaurant.

"Oh great," he said, as the theater director started toward them.

"Who's that?" Veronica asked.

"Milton, the theater man from Blackhawk."

"Mr. Adams," Milton said. "So glad to see you out and about. Is your game over?"

"Far from it," Clint said. "We're just taking a break for supper. From here we'll be playing twenty-four hours until somebody wins."

"I see," Milton said. He looked at Bat and Veronica, who Clint didn't bother to introduce. "I'll leave you to it, then. But when you are done, I hope you'll make time to dine with me. I have a proposition."

"We'll have to see about that," Clint said.

"Enjoy your meal," Milton said, and went to a table to dine alone.

"What do you think his proposition is going to be?" Veronica asked.

"I don't have any idea," Clint said, "and I'm not sure I care."

"You don't like that man one bit," she said.

"Did it show that much?" he asked with a smile, as their meals arrived.

Chapter Twenty-Eight

Fortified for what lay ahead, Clint, Bat and Veronica returned to the Blue Rose. The final table was set up in the center of the back room. A small bar had been set up against the wall, to keep the players supplied with whatever they wanted—whiskey, beer, brandy, coffee. And even sarsaparilla. Wilford Tweedy stood by the table. There were also two of Tweedy's security men standing nearby, armed with shotguns. The two saloon girls were also there, to service the players. They wore a blue and a green dress, respectively.

"Let's all be seated," Tweedy said.

The players sat. Clint was seated across from Bat, with Veronica to his right.

"We all understand there are no more breaks," Tweedy said. "You arc permitted to go to the bar to collect a drink, or one of the girls will bring it to you. But you can't be away from the table for more than ten minutes."

"I'll depend on my girls to bring me my drinks," Johnny Dark said with a smile.

All their chips had been stacked for them. The largest were in front of Bat and Veronica. Clint's was the next highest, Mattingly's and Kenyon's were about the same. For the moment, they were all well ahead. There was six hundred thousand dollars on the table. For all but Bat, it was the biggest game any of them had ever taken part in.

Tweedy himself placed a card in front of each of them. The high card went to Veronica.

"Deal!" Tweedy said.

***

After supper at the Sawyer House, E.P. Milton took a walk around town. He was looking for a likely building to use as a theater while he was having a new one built, if his ultimate plan came to fruition.

The townspeople he passed along the way had no idea who he was. Some ignored him, and some exchanged a brief nod. As he walked, he thought about the woman who had been sitting with Clint Adams. She was beautiful and had the most amazing blue eyes. Even though most of the audience would not be able to see her eyes on stage, he still felt that she had a presence that would work in the theater. He hoped to find out who she was from Clint Adams, and perhaps gain an introduction. But his main goal was still Adams himself. He hoped that the man would have a large enough ego that he would go for the pitch Milton was planning. And it had very little to do with Kit Dalton's demand that he set up a shooting match between them.

***

In the sheriff's office, Wood sat at his desk with a mug of strong coffee from the pot sitting on his pot-bellied stove.

Milton had not been overly impressed with the opera house, which suited Wood quite well. But the man had other plans that the lawman was not aware of. And Milton had asked Wood to set up a meeting for him with the town's mayor. Wood had only just returned from the mayor's office . . .

***

. . . "What does he want?" Mayor Morris Williams asked.

Williams had been the mayor of Central City for six years. He was in his second term.

"He didn't say," Wood said, "but I'm sure it has somethin' to do with building a theater here in town."

"He's doing quite well in Blackhawk," the mayor observed.

"Blackhawks' bigger than us," Wood said, "and needed somethin' with the mines playin' out."

"You forget, Harvey," Morris said, "our mines are also playing out."

"Yeah, but a theater?" Wood asked. "We have enough trouble operatin' the opera house."

"That may be," the mayor said, "but Milton would be operating the theater. And he wouldn't be asking us for money, would he?"

"I don't know what he's gonna ask for."

"Well," Morris said, "maybe we should find out. I'll see him tomorrow morning . . ."

***

Sheriff Wood had not yet told Milton he had his meeting with the mayor. He thought he would wait til morning to do that. By then maybe the man would have seen enough of Central City to change his mind.

Chapter Twenty-Nine

For the first two hours the six players pretty much played evenly. Then the stack of chips in front of Mattingly began to dwindle. His final hand found him opposing both Johnny Dark and Veronica. The hand involved several raises, until ultimately all of Mattingly's chips were in the pot.

"I'll just call," Veronica said, "since you're out of chips."

"Same here," Johnny said. "We've both called your last raise, Mattingly. What've you got?"

The hand was five card stud. Mattingly turned his cards over. "Full house, Kings over threes."

"That beats me," Johnny said, turning his own full house over, Jacks over sevens.

"Ouch," Veronica said. "Sorry, boys."

She turned her cards over, revealing four eights.

"Wow," Mattingly said, "that busts me." He stood. "Good luck to you all."

As Mattingly walked away, Johnny said, "That leaves one more of us to go."

"Yes," Kenyon said, "then two of us will walk away with forty grand."

"Better than losing," Veronica said.

"Not if you were counting on winning," Kenyon said, "and I am. Deal!"

***

Milton was very pleased to see the sheriff at his door the next morning.

"You have your meetin' with the mayor," Wood said.

"Excellent! When?"

"In an hour," Wood said. "You have time for breakfast."

"Good. I'll have that here in the hotel. Would you care to join me?"

"Why not?" Wood said.

There wasn't much conversation between them as they ate, and then they left and walked to City Hall, where Woods made the introductions.

"Very happy to meet you, Mr. Milton," Mayor Morris said. "I've heard wonderful things about what you've been doing in Blackhawk."

"Thank you, Mr. Mayor."

"Please, have a seat," Morris said. "Sheriff, that'll be all."

Wood didn't like being dismissed that way, but withdrew and left the two men to discuss the theatrical downfall of Central City.

"I understand you wanted to see me," the mayor said. "What's it about?"

"To put it bluntly, I'd like to build a theater here in Central City. I'd like to bring some culture here, much the way I did in Blackhawk."

"Central City is not a place where I'd think culture would thrive," the mayor said. "We have enough trouble keeping our opera house going."

"I'd think so," Milton said. "It doesn't look like much is being done in the way of keeping it up."

"Believe me," Morris said, "an opera house wasn't my idea."

"Who's idea was it?"

"Someone who doesn't even live here anymore," the mayor said. "He built it, left town, and now we're stuck with it. Say, why not just turn the opera house into your theater?"

"I envision something very different," Milton said. "I just want to make sure there's no opposition from your office."

"I don't oppose anything that won't cost the town money," Morris said.

"Don't worry about that," Milton said. "I won't be asking you for any money."

"Then you have my blessing," Mayor Morris said. "Where would you like to put this theater of yours?"

"I'm still looking for a good location," Milton said, "but I have an idea for attracting attention."

"Anything you can tell me now?"

"No," Milton said, "I'm still working on that, as well."

"Then if that's all—"

"Yes, yes," Milton said, "I imagine a politician such as yourself has a lot of work to do. I'll let you get to it."

Milton stood up and both men shook hands.

"Please," Morris said, "keep me informed on your progress."

"I will, sir. Thank you for your time."

Milton left City Hall, now assured of no interference.

***

Next to bust out of the game was Johnny Dark. It came down to a hand between him and Veronica. They bet, raised and re-raised until Johnny pushed the remainder of his chips in.

"That's it, Blue Eyes," he said. "All my chips."

"Then I'll call," she said.

Johnny turned his cards over.

"Three ladies," he said, revealing his Queens.

"Three Kings," Veronica said, turning her cards over. "Sorry Johnny."

"Don't be," Johnny said, standing, "at least I lost to those blue eyes. Good luck, everyone."

"We're down to four," Kenyon said.

Clint knew that Bat was sitting back, allowing the other players to take each other out. Now that they were down to four, Bat would start playing in earnest . . .

***

It soon became obvious that the cards were going to do the talking. None of the players was going to be bluffed out of a hand. Not with the amount of money that was on the line. So when somebody raised, they actually had the cards. This meant the game was down to the luck of the draw, and not the skill of the players.

And even Veronica's blue eyes were not a factor.

Bat was dealing a hand of five card stud, when it came down to Kenyon and Veronica having all their chips in the pot, with four cards on the table and one still to come.

"All your chips are in," Bat said, "so no more bets. Fifth card coming out."

He dealt Kenyon a Four of Spades, giving him a pair of fours, and Veronica a Queen of Hearts, giving her a pair of Queens showing.

"That's it," Bat said, putting the deck down. "Show time."

Veronica turned over her hole card. It was a Jack of Hearts, which matched a Jack of Clubs on the table. She had two pair, Queens and Jacks.

"Two pair," Bat said. "Kenyon?"

Kenyon turned over his hole card. It was a third four.

"Trip fours," Bat said. "Kenyon wins, Lady Poker is out."

"That was quite a play," Veronica said to him.

"Just a hunch," Kenyon said. "And I was feeling lucky."

Wilford Tweedy had been watching from the bar. He now came forward and said, "Miss Belmont has gone bust. She's out in fourth place for forty grand."

"Gentlemen," Veronica said with a smile, "best of luck."

"The game continues," Tweedy said, and walked back to the bar. Veronica followed him there.

"May I stay and watch?" she asked.

"Of course. Drink?"

"Brandy, please."

It was now down to Clint, Bat and Kenyon. Their chip stacks were roughly even. At this point the game became more cutthroat, as if having the lady out changed the tone. Suddenly, bluffing became a big part of the game, as the men tried to read each other. Clint knew Bat had no tells, but he was studying Kenyon to see if he could pick anything up. He took one hand from the man with a pair of deuces over an Ace high. Earlier in the game, neither of them would have played such a hand.

"Very nice," Kenyon said, as Clint raked in the chips.

"Just lucky," Clint said.

Chapter Thirty

It's generally understood that in a two-handed game, money simply goes back-and-forth. A two-handed game can go on forever unless the players start taking chances. This game was now three-handed, but the rule still followed. The money would go back-and-forth, and the game would go on for days unless somebody started taking chances.

Bat Masterson was the one who started taking chances. He could read Clint and Kenyon, and he seemed to know when he could bluff, or when he could convince them he was bluffing. His chip stacks started to grow, and theirs started to dwindle. By the break for supper, he had more chips than they did, combined.

There wasn't supposed to be a meal break, but Tweedy came to the table and said, "I think you boys could use a break. Why not go and get something to eat?"

"Sounds good," Clint said.

"Why not?" Kenyon said.

Bat was on a roll, so he grumbled but agreed. The three men stood up.

"My men'll be here with the chips," Tweedy assured them.

Veronica came over and said, "Do you gentlemen mind if I join you?"

"It would be our pleasure," Bat said.

They left the Blue Rose and walked to the Sawyer House. Outside, Kenyon stopped.

"This place is a little too highfalutin for me," he said. "I'll see you back at the game?"

He turned and walked off.

"Funny," Veronica said, as they entered, "he didn't seem that type."

"That's what I was thinking," Clint said.

"To each his own," Bat said.

As they were shown to a table, Clint saw E.P. Milton sitting and eating alone.

"Order me a steak, will you?" he said to Bat. "I want to see what this fellow has on his mind."

"Sure thing."

Clint walked over to Milton's table.

"Mind if I sit?" he asked.

"Not at all," Milton said. "Join me—"

"Just for a moment," Clint said, sitting. "What was the idea of trying to get me tossed in a jail cell?"

"That was a mistake," Milton said. "I just wanted to make sure you were here when I arrived. I didn't know how long your poker game would last."

"Why'd you want me to be here? What's on your mind?"

"You are, Mr. Adams," Milton said, putting his utensils down. "I have a proposition for you."

"So you said."

"Kit Dalton wants to shoot against you in the show."

"Not a chance."

"Wait til you hear my offer."

"It doesn't matter," Clint said. "I'm not interested in humbling that girl on a stage, in front of people."

"You're sure you can beat her?" Milton said.

"You forget, I've seen her shoot. She's not bad for your stage, but she wouldn't stand a chance against me or any other professional. And my advice is not to let her try. It might destroy her self-confidence, and then you've lost a performer."

"I see," Milton said. "You're probably right. Thanks for the advice."

"So if there's nothing else . . ." Clint said, starting to rise.

"But there is," Milton said.

Clint sat back down.

"Yes?"

"I want to build a theater here in Central City," Milton said, "and I want you to be my star attraction."

"I'm not interested in the theater."

"But not only my attraction," Milton said, "I want to name the theater after you. The Gunsmith Theater. I'd pay you very well."

Clint doubted the man could match what he might win in the poker game.

"Still not interested," Clint said. "I especially don't want my name on a theater or any other business." He had recently turned down having a brewery named after him in Kentucky.

"But you'd be a star," Milton said. "I can guarantee it."

"Mr. Milton," Clint said, "the answer is no."

"But . . . if you don't agree, I don't think I can go ahead with the project. And this town would benefit greatly from a theater."

"I doubt that," Clint said. "I think what you mean is, you'd benefit greatly from it."

"And you!"

Clint stood up.

"I'm not interested in having my name on your theater or being a fool on your stage. Enjoy your meal."

Clint stood and went over to join Veronica and Bat.

"What was on his mind?" Bat asked.

"You wouldn't believe it."

Chapter Thirty-One

When Clint, Bat and Veronica got back to the Blue Rose, neither Kenyon nor Tweedy were there.

"Where's Tweedy?" Bat asked a bartender.

"Haven't seen him."

Bat looked at Clint. They walked to the curtained doorway to look in the back room. The chips were on the table, with two of Tweedy's shotgun guards, but no sign of Tweedy. They went back to the small bar in the room.

"Where's the boss?"

"Haven't seen him," the bartender said.

Clint went to the two shotgun guards.

"You boys seen Tweedy?"

"Not since you all left," one of them said.

Veronica came through the curtain.

"I talked to the two girls. They haven't seen him."

"What about Kenyon?" Bat asked the bartender. "Any sign of him?"

"Not since you all left."

Clint looked at the table. All the chips were there, but they were just chips.

"Where's the money?" he asked the two guards.

"In a safe in the boss's office, upstairs."

"Any guards on it?"

"Yeah, a couple."

Clint joined Bat at the bar.

"Are you thinking what I'm thinking?" he asked his friend.

"I hope not," Bat said. "I thought Tweedy was on the level."

"There's one way to find out," Clint said.

"Right," Bat said.

They looked at Veronica and Clint said, "You better stay in the saloon."

"Where are you boys going?" she asked.

"To pay our host a visit," Clint said.

They all left the back room to go into the saloon. Veronica took a seat at an empty table. Clint and Bat walked over to the stairs. A burly shotgun guard barred their way.

"Can't go up," he said.

"We want to see Tweedy," Bat said.

"He'll be down soon."

"He should've been down already," Clint said. "We're ready to start and we're missing a player."

"Sorry," the guard said, "can't let you go up."

"We're not asking you to let us up," Bat said.

"We're *telling* you we're going up," Clint said.

The guard tried to stand his ground but looking into the eyes of Bat Masterson and the Gunsmith, he finally stepped aside.

Chapter Thirty-Two

On the second floor Clint said, "Which one's his office?"

"I don't know," Bat said. "Let's try them all."

The first two rooms they tried were unlocked, and turned out to be rooms where the girls would entertain. The third door was locked.

"This has got to be the one," Bat said.

They knocked, but there was no answer.

"Allow me," Clint said. He backed up, then kicked out at the door. His boot heel hit just below the knob and the door snapped open.

They entered the room and stopped. There was a desk, a chair, and a five-foot high safe. Also, a guard with a shotgun, who had apparently been dozing in the chair. He jumped to his feet, eyes wide.

"Where's the boss?" Clint asked.

"Don't know. Whataya mean by kickin' the door in?" he demanded. "And how'd you get up here? Wasn't Stan at the bottom of the steps?"

"Yes," Bat said, "we managed to convince Stan to let us come up."

"When's the last time you saw your boss?" Clint asked.

"Earlier today," the guard said. "What's goin' on?"

"That's what we want to know," Bat said. "Has that safe been opened today?"

The guard looked at it, then said, "I dunno. Not since I been here."

"Who has the combination?" Bat asked.

"Just the boss."

Clint walked to the safe and tried the handle. The door didn't budge.

It's locked," Clint said to Bat. "We might be jumping the gun."

"Maybe," Bat said, "but where's Kenyon?" Bat asked. "He must've had a reason not to eat with us."

"We might be misjudging them both," Clint said, "but it's too much of a coincidence that neither one's here."

"Maybe," Bat said, "but there's a lot of money involved. Tweedy may have wanted the whole six hundred thousand, and not his two hundred thousand cut."

"What's that got to do with Kenyon not being here?" Clint asked. "Maybe Kenyon's got Tweedy."

"But where's the money?" Bat asked. "I want a look inside this safe."

"Let's check the desk," Clint said. "Maybe the combination's written down."

The guard stepped in front of the desk.

"I can't let ya do that," he said.

"Look," Bat said, "something's wrong. Two men are missing. We just want to make sure the money's still here."

"So either move aside," Clint said, "or we'll move you."

The guard hesitated, then moved.

"Sorry" Clint told him, but your boss may be in trouble."

Bat went through all the drawers in the desk and came up empty.

"Nothing," he said.

"He would have been a fool to leave it written down in the desk," Clint said. "Tweedy doesn't strike me as a fool."

"But fool enough to steal the money?" Bat asked.

"Whata you talkin' about, steal?" the guard said. "I thought you said he was in trouble."

"He's in trouble if somebody else stole the money," Bat said.

"He's in trouble with *us* if he stole it," Clint added.

"Jesus," the guard said.

"Tweedy must have a number two man," Bat said. "Who would that be?" He turned toward the guard.

The guard said, "I dunno, maybe Ike Reynolds."

"Who's that?" Bat asked.

"One of the bartenders downstairs," the guard said. "The older one."

"Has he been up here today?"

"Not while I been here."

"What's your name?"

"They call me Ditch."

"Ditch?" Bat said. "Why?"

The man looked embarrassed.

"My real name's Dudley, and I hate it."

"Okay, Ditch," Bat said. "You stay on guard here until Mr. Adams or I say so."

"B-but . . . why?"

Bat stared at him and said, "Because I say so."

"Yeah, okay," Ditch said.

Bat looked at Clint.

"Let's have a word with Ike."

"Right."

They left the room, couldn't lock the door because Clint's kick had broken the lock. But that safe would keep anyone out who didn't have the combination, and Ditch was convinced to remain on guard.

Chapter Thirty-Three

Downstairs Veronica started to rise when they came down, but they waved her away and went to the bar. Of the two bartenders, it wasn't hard to tell the difference. One was in his late twenties, one in his fifties.

"Are you Ike?" Clint asked him.

"That's me."

He had told them earlier that he hadn't seen the boss.

"We understand you're Mr. Tweedy's right-hand man."

"Who told you that?"

"Ditch," Bat said.

"Ditch has a big mouth," Ike said. "What's on your mind?"

"Our third player's not here, and neither is your boss," Bat said. "What's going on?"

"You got me," Ike said. "I'm a bartender. The poker challenge is all Tweedy's."

"In that case, we'd like to get a look inside his safe," Clint said.

"Why?"

"We want to make sure the challenge money is there," Bat said.

"Why wouldn't it be?" Ike asked.

"You tell us," Bat said. "Why would Tweedy not be here to restart the game?"

"Beats me," Ike said. "Maybe he found a woman."

"Look," Clint said, "he's either in trouble and needs our help, or he's gone, and so is the money."

"Naw, the boss wouldn't do that," Ike said.

"Then help us find him," Clint said. "But first, do you know the combination to the safe in his office?"

"I sure don't," Ike said. "The boss keeps that to himself."

"If we can't get a look inside that safe," Clint said to Bat, "we don't know what we're chasing."

"Why chase anythin'?" Ike asked.

"What do you mean?"

"There's still two of you," the bartender said. "If the third player doesn't appear, the two of you can continue. You still have your chips. You can divide the third players' chips evenly."

"Are you empowered to make that decision?" Bat asked.

"Well, like you said," Ike replied, "I'm Mr. Tweedy's right-hand man. If he's not here, I guess I'm in charge until he returns."

"*If* he returns," Bat said.

"We can get the sheriff to look for him and the third player, while you two continue."

"I don't have much faith in your local law," Bat said. He looked at Clint. "I say we suspend play while we try to find either Kenyon, or Tweedy. The chips can stay where they are, under guard."

"If there's no money in that safe," Clint said, "those chips are worthless. And if the money's gone, and Tweedy's gone, it's obvious what happened. He conned us all and lit out with the money."

"I still can't believe that," Ike said.

"Can you instruct those shotgun guards to keep doing their job?" Bat asked.

"I can," Ike said. "They'll listen to me."

"Okay," Clint said, "the two in the back room, the one on the stairs, and the one in the office. Keep them there."

"And what are you going to do?" Ike asked.

"We're going to find Kenyon, or Tweedy. Personally, I'd rather find Tweedy. Does he live upstairs?"

"He's got the office, and a room where he sleeps," Ike said, "but he's also got a house at the north end of town. It's got a white picket fence in front, and it's one level."

"Does anyone else live there?"

"He's got a woman," Ike said. "She takes care of the house, and him, when he's there. Her name's Gloria."

"If he was leaving town, would he take her with him?" Bat asked.

"Probably not," Ike said. "She's like these girls here, just doing a job."

"Okay," Clint said. "Ike, we expect to find you here when we get back."

"If you're not here, we'll know you lied to us, and we'll be looking for you, too," Bat added.

"I understand."

Clint and Bat walked over to Veronica and told her what was going on.

"Why don't you try to get into the safe?" she asked. "We really don't know what's going on until we know the money's still there."

"We could blow it," Clint said. "But too little dynamite won't work, and too much could blow up the money, if it's there."

"You might as well go back to your hotel, Veronica," Bat said. "Get some rest and wait there. If and when the game continues, we'll come and let you know so you can watch."

"All right," she said. "But be careful."

She started away and Bat said, "Veronica."

"Yes?"

"How do you know we won't take the money and run?"

She smiled.

"I trust you both, Bat," she said. "You're both honest men."

She turned and left the saloon.

As Clint and Bat were preparing to leave, Johnny Dark came over.

"What's goin' on?" he asked. "Why aren't you playin'?"

They explained the situation to him, and he listened intently.

"That sonofabitch!" he seethed. "If he took the money, then he flimflammed all of us. I'm comin' with you."

"I've got a better idea," Clint said. "We can't be sure if Ike, the bartender, is telling us the truth. When we leave, he might run."

"You want me to sit on 'im?"

"For as long as you can," Clint said, "but if you have to face some of them, then let him go. Don't get yourself killed."

"Don't worry," Johnny said. "He's not going nowhere."

Clint and Bat left the Blue Rose and headed to the north of town.

"How do you think this is going to end?" Bat asked Clint.

"I'm determined that it's going to end the way we want," Clint said. "With you having the money for your casino in San Francisco."

Chapter Thirty-Four

They found Wilford Tweedy's house. They opened the gate of the picket fence and walked to the door. If Tweedy was there, he had a lot of explaining to do. They knocked on the door and waited. It was answered by a lovely woman in her early thirties, wearing a plain, cotton dress. Her hair was long but tied back out of her eyes. She looked as if she had been cleaning.

"Yes?"

"Are you Gloria?" Clint asked. "Is this Wilford Tweedy's house?"

"I am, and it is," she said. "What can I do for you?"

"I'm Clint Adams, and this is Bat Masterson."

"Oh, you're two of the poker players," she said. "Wilford has talked about you. Why aren't you playing?"

"That's our problem," Clint said. "Our third player has disappeared, and apparently so has Tweedy. Do you know where he is?"

"I thought he was at the Blue Rose."

"He's not," Bat said. "I'm sure you can see why we're concerned."

"I'm afraid I don't," she said. "Can't you continue the game without him?"

"We need to find our third player," Clint said. "But before we continue, we want to find out if we'll be continuing to play in vain."

"I still don't understand?"

"May we come in?" Clint asked.

"I would've invited you, but I'm in the middle of cleaning." She stepped outside and closed the door. "We can talk out here."

"All right," Bat said. "Our problem is, we don't know if the poker money is in the safe or not."

"If it's not in the safe, where would it—oh, I think I see. You're afraid Wilford has stolen the money."

"He called a break for supper, even though there wasn't supposed to be one," Clint said. "During the break, he may have stolen the money and left town."

"That's impossible," Gloria said. "He'd never leave without me."

"Are you sure of that?" Clint asked. "We were told that you're just an employee, like the girls in the saloon."

"That's not quite true," she said. "You see, I'm Wilford's wife."

"His wife?" Bat said. "We didn't know he was married."

"No one does. So you see, he wouldn't have left without me."

"Not even for six hundred thousand dollars?"

"Wilford loves me, and he loves his saloon," she said. "He wouldn't leave either one, for any amount of money."

"We'd like to believe that," Clint said. "Gloria—Mrs. Tweedy—"

"You can call me Gloria."

"Gloria, we'd like to come in and look around."

"Do you think I'm hiding my husband here?"

"We just want to be sure," Bat said, "before we go looking elsewhere."

"Well . . . I suppose it's all right." She opened the door. "Go ahead."

"Thank you."

The house was well furnished, but at the moment in a state of disarray from her cleaning. They split up and searched the house thoroughly. In the bedroom all of Tweedy's clothes seemed to be there, but there was no sign of Wilford Tweedy, himself.

"Are you satisfied?" Gloria asked, as they came back into the living room.

"That he's not here, yes," Bat said. "Not that he hasn't stolen the money."

"Gloria, do you have the combination to his office safe?"

She didn't answer right away, which was, in itself, an answer.

"We need to see what's in that safe," Clint said.

"I don't know—"

"If there's no money there, don't you want to know if he took it and left town?" Bat asked."

"And if the money is there," Clint said, "then he might be in trouble."

"We'd like to know if we're looking for him to rescue him, or arrest him," Bat said.

"You don't have the authority—"

"If the money's not there, we'll bring the law in," Clint told her.

"All right, very well," she said. "I have the combination. But I want to come with you."

"That's fine," Bat said.

She left the room and came back with a slip of paper in her hand.

"This is the combination." Bat reached for it, but she pulled it back. "I'm coming, remember? I'll open the safe."

"All right," Bat said, drawing his hand back.

"Gloria," Clint said. "Do you know a man named Kenyon?"

"I don't believe so."

"He's never been here?" Bat asked. "Your husband never mentioned him?"

"No, not that I remember."

"All right, then," Clint said. "Let's get to that safe."

Chapter Thirty-Five

When Clint and Bat walked into the saloon with Gloria, Ike was still behind the bar, serving drinks. Johnny Dark was sitting at a table with his buddy, Bill Hager. They walked to the stairs, which were being guarded but the same shotgun guard.

"Ma'am."

"It's all right, Chuck. They're with me."

"Yes, Ma'am."

The guard stepped aside, and they went up. When they got to the broken door, the guard also stepped aside. Inside, Ditch got up out of his chair.

"Ma'am," he said.

"Hello, Ditch."

"Did you find the boss?" he asked Clint.

"No, that's why we're here with Gloria. She's going to open the safe."

"I guess that's all right, then," Ditch said.

"If the money's in there, we're still going to need you to guard it," Bat said.

"Yes, sir."

Gloria went to the safe and, reading the combination off the slip of paper in her hand, she opened it.

***

E.P. Milton was not happy after his exchange with Clint Adams. The man was a fool not to take advantage of an opportunity like this. Milton was convinced he could make a bigger showman than Buffalo Bill Cody out of Adams. He had to convince Adams of that, somehow.

Milton figured that the most influential man in Central City was the owner of the Blue Rose Saloon, Wilford Tweedy. He'd had several good exchanges with Tweedy over the past six months. He was hoping the man would be on his side when it came to building a theater. He hadn't yet spoken to the man this trip, because he was occupied with his poker tournament. But when that business was over, he would approach Tweedy. With his help he felt sure he could get what he wanted. He decided to have a talk with Sheriff Wood to see what was going on in town.

***

Gloria Tweedy swung the safe door open and then stared at the inside, stunned.

"Well?" Clint asked.

She turned her head to look at him.

"It's empty."

"What?" Bat darted forward to have a look, then straightened and looked at Clint.

"No money," he said. "It's gone."

Clint turned to Ditch.

"Don't look at me," the guard said. "The safe was locked when I came on duty. As far as I knew, the money was there."

"He took it," Clint said. "Tweedy's taken off with the money."

"Why did Kenyon not want to eat with us?" Bat asked. "Is he involved, as well?"

"If he stands pat, he comes in third, he makes forty thousand," Bat pointed out.

"But if he's working with Tweedy, he gets a lot more than that."

"I don't believe it," Gloria said. "Something's wrong."

"Something's wrong, all right," Clint said. "Ditch, who did you relieve?"

"Eddie Call."

"Where is he now?"

"I assume he's home, asleep."

"So the money had to be removed before you came on duty," Bat said.

"Eddie?" Ditch asked,

"Working with your boss," Clint said.

Bat asked Clint, "How do you want to play this?"

"You said you would bring in the law," Gloria reminded him. "If my husband's in trouble, I want the sheriff working on this."

"One of us has to talk to Eddie Call, and the other can go to the sheriff with Gloria."

"I would like Mr. Masterson to go with me," Gloria said, then looked at Clint and added, "no offense."

"None taken," Clint said.

"How do we know where Call lives?" Bat asked.

"Ditch can take one of us there," Clint said, looking at the guard.

"Oh, yeah, sure," Ditch said. "I know where Eddie lives."

"What do we tell the others?" Bat asked. "Veronica, Johnny, the other guards."

"The truth," Clint said. "The money's gone, and so is Wilford Tweedy."

"You won't say he stole the money, will you?" Gloria asked. "I mean, we don't know that's true."

"Gloria," Clint said, "we're going to find out what *is* true."

Chapter Thirty-Six

Clint followed Ditch to a rooming house in the center of town. It was two floors, with a well painted exterior.

"This is Ma Freeling's house," Ditch said. "She has a few of the guards here."

They mounted the porch and knocked. An elderly, grey-haired woman answered.

"Dudley," she said. "And who's this?"

"This is Clint Adams, Ma'am," Ditch said. "He's here to see Eddie Call."

"I believe Mr. Call is still asleep," the woman said.

"I'm sorry, Ma'am," Clint said, "but it's necessary for us to wake him up."

She heaved a sigh and said, "If you say so, Dudley."

"Yes, Ma'am."

She swung the door wide and said, "Go ahead, then."

Clint and Ditch entered the house, and Ditch led the way to the stairs.

***

Bat opened the door to the sheriff's office for Gloria to precede him.

"Mr. Masterson," Wood said. "Gloria. What can I do for you?"

"Wilford Tweedy is missing," Bat said.

"Is that true?"

"It is," Gloria said, "and I'm worried."

"That's not all," Bat said. "The poker money is missing, also."

Wood looked surprised.

"How much is that?"

"Six hundred thousand."

"Good God!" Wood blurted.

"And another player named Kenyon is also missing," Bat finished.

"What do you want me to do?" Wood asked.

"I want you to find my husband," Gloria said. "I believe he's in trouble."

Wood looked at Bat.

"And you think he stole the money?"

"There's a good chance."

"With the help of this other man, Kenyon?" Woods asked.

"Possibly."

"No," Gloria said. "Wilford wouldn't do that. He's in trouble."

"Gloria," Sheriff Wood said, "I think you'd have a better chance of findin' him than I do. I wouldn't know where to start lookin'."

"You could start," Bat said, "by going wherever he stores his horse and seeing if it's still there."

"See?" Woods said to Gloria. "You and Masterson can find him before I do."

"But you're the law!" Gloria said.

"And I've got a prisoner here I'm responsible for," Woods said. "I can't just leave."

Gloria looked at the man, then at Bat.

"Where does he store his horse?" Bat asked.

"I can show you," Gloria said.

"Then let's go."

They left the sheriff's office, now convinced he would be no help.

***

Ditch and Clint went up the stairs and down the hall to a closed door. Clint knocked. There was no answer.

"He's a sound sleeper," Ditch said.

Clint pounded on the door.

"Not that sound," he said. "Let's force it."

Together they pressed their shoulders to the door until the lock popped and the door swung open. Inside, there was a man lying on the bed. He was a bloody mess.

Clint walked to the bed for a better look.

"He's dead," he said. "Is this Call?"

Ditch walked to the bed and said, "Yeah, that's him."

"We better fetch the sheriff," Clint said.

Chapter Thirty-Seven

Ditch went for the sheriff while Clint remained with the body. The man's clothes and shotgun were in a corner. From what Clint could see, his throat had been cut.

"Oh, my . . ."

Clint turned and saw the old lady standing at the door.

"How could this have happened?" she demanded.

"That's what I'd like to know."

"This is horrible."

"Yes, it is."

"Who's going to pay for my sheets?" she asked.

"I think you better go downstairs, Ma'am," Clint told her.

She turned and walked away.

When Ditch returned with the sheriff, the lawman stared at the body.

"Does this have something to do with the missin' money?" he asked Clint.

"The missing money, and the missing men," Clint said. "I'm sure of it."

"Well," Wood said, "like I told Masterson and Mrs. Tweedy, you three have the best chance of findin' whoever did this and stole the money."

"You're not going to do anything?" Clint asked.

"I have a prisoner to watch."

"As far as I'm concerned," Clint said, "this is more important than the prisoner. Let him go."

"I'm holdin' him til the circuit judge gets here," Wood said. "That's my job."

"This is your job, too," Clint said.

"Findin' a killer?" Wood asked. "I'm no detective."

"Where did Bat and Gloria go after they left your office?" Clint asked.

"They went to see if Tweedy's horse was still in the livery."

"I should go and join them, then," Clint said. "What about this body?"

"I can have it moved to the undertaker's."

"Good," Clint said. "At least you'll do that."

"Have you talked to that theater fella, Milton?" Wood asked.

"Yes," Clint said, "but I don't have time for him."

"Maybe you should take time."

"Why's that?"

"He's associated with Mr. Tweedy."

"I didn't know that," Clint said. "Thanks."

He started to leave, then turned back and said, "You better talk with the landlady, here."

"Why?"

"She wants someone to pay for her sheets," Clint said, and left to find Ditch downstairs.

"Do you know where Tweedy kept his horse?" he asked.

"Yeah, in a livery stable at the end of main street."

"Take me there."

"Okay." As they left the house Ditch asked, "Do you know if I'm still gettin' paid?"

"That's another reason for us to find Tweedy," Clint said.

***

As Ditch led Clint to the livery stable, Bat and Gloria were coming out.

"Anything?" Clint asked.

"His horse is gone," Bat said. "All the more reason to believe he stole the money."

"I still can't believe it," Gloria said.

"That he stole six hundred thousand dollars?" Clint asked her.

"No," she said, shaking her head, "that he would leave without me."

"I'm going to take her back to her house," Bat said.

"I'll take a look inside," Clint said. "We'll need something to identify his tracks."

"I'll meet you back at the Blue Rose," Bat said.

"Okay."

"What do I do?" Ditch asked.

"You're free to go," Clint said. "You have a room?"

"I do."

"Go there," Clint said. "Relax. If we find Tweedy and the money and bring them back, you'll know."

"I think I'll go to the Blue Rose," Ditch said, "tell the other guards what's going on."

"Good idea," Clint said. "I'll see you there."

They all split up and Clint went into the livery. He spoke to the hostler, who told him which stall Tweedy's horse had been in. He studied the ground in the stall, looking for an identifying mark in the horse's tracks.

"There," he said to the hostler, "see that? A star shaped mark in the center."

"It's a scar," the hostler said. "I remember the horse went lame one time, stepped on a stone. It cut the soft part of its hoof and later heeled. That must be the scar."

"That's it, then," Clint said.

This was the same livery where Clint had boarded his Tobiano when he arrived in town.

"I'll need my horse," he said.

"When?" the hostler asked.

"Tomorrow morning," Clint said, "there's no point in riding out tonight. It'll soon be pitch dark."

"I'll have 'im ready."

"Is Masterson's horse here?" Clint asked.

"No," the hostler said, "it must be in the other stable, at the other end of town."

"Okay," Clint said. "Thanks."

He left the livery and started walking to the Blue Rose.

Chapter Thirty-Eight

When Clint walked into the Blue Rose, Bat was seated at a table with a beer. Clint walked over and joined him. Before he could say a word, one of the girls came over.

"Drink?" she asked.

"Yes, a beer," Clint said.

"Comin' up."

She hurried to the bar. The other patrons were looking at him and Bat, and he wondered if they knew what was going on. The shotgun guards who were in the place were gone.

"I checked the back," Bat said. "The chips are still on the table."

"What good are they?" Clint asked.

"Well," Bat said, "if we can get the money back, we might continue the game."

"Or," Clint said, "we could spit the pot three ways. That would still give you enough for your casino. In fact, I'd invest some of mine."

"That sounds good," Bat said. "And without Kenyon we'd be splitting it two ways. We could even give Veronica some."

"And Johnny Dark," Clint said.

"We can discuss it," Bat said. "First we have to find Tweedy and the money."

"How was Gloria when you left her?"

"I think she's in shock," Bat said. "We should probably send a doctor to see her."

"If there's one in town."

"What'd you find at the stable?"

"A mark we can use to identify the tracks," Clint said.

"Luckily you're a better tracker than I am."

"I figure we'll head out in the morning," Clint said.

"I'm fine with that."

"But I have an idea."

"What is it?"

"Sheriff Wood told me that the theater man, Milton, knew Tweedy."

"You think he'd know where he is?"

"I don't know," Clint said, "but it's worth asking him."

"You know where he's staying?"

"The Dundee."

"You want to do it tonight?"

"Why not?" Clint asked. "What else is there to do? And while we're there, we can fill Veronica in on what's happened."

Bat looked over at the bar, saw the older bartender watching them.

"Maybe we should fill Ike in, as well," Bat said. "If Tweedy doesn't come back, this place'll go to his wife, and she'll need Ike to run it."

They finished their beers and then left to go to the Dundee Hotel. At the desk they asked for Milton's room number, then climbed the stairs and knocked. When the man opened the door, he looked surprised.

"Mr. Adams," he said. "And . . . a friend?"

"Bat Masterson's my name," Bat said.

"Well," Milton said, "prestigious company. What can I do for you gents?"

"Can we come in?" Clint asked. "We'd like to ask you some questions."

"Why not?" Milton said. "I'm not doing anything."

He allowed them to enter and then closed the door.

"I have a bottle of brandy here, if you're interested," he said.

"No, thank you," Clint said.

Bat shook his head. He stood back and allowed Clint to take the lead.

"We wanted to ask you about your relationship with Wilford Tweedy," Clint said.

"Mr. Tweedy?" Milton said. "Well, I've met him a time or two. Why?"

"He seems to have disappeared."

"Disappeared? Really? He seems to be quite a successful businessman in town. Where could he have gone?"

"That's what we're trying to find out," Clint said. He decided to keep the missing money part of the story to himself, for now. Bat seemed to go along.

"But . . . why ask me?"

"I thought you might be friends," Clint said, "both of you being successful businessmen in their area."

"I haven't even seen him since I got here," Milton said. "Although I was thinking of stopping in on him before leaving town."

"Are you leaving?"

"Not quite yet," Milton said. "I still have some looking around to do."

"For a location for your theater?" Bat asked.

"I'm still considering the possibility, yes," Milton said.

"Well," Clint said, "we'll say good night, then."

"Yes, good night to you both."

He opened the door for them and immediately closed it.

"Couldn't get rid of us fast enough," Bat said.

"You think?"

"I might as well go to my room, since we're here," Bat said.

"Yes, I'll go to my hotel and turn in," Clint said. "Let's do breakfast tomorrow before we start out."

"See you then."

Bat went to his room, and Clint left the Dundee Hotel, deciding not to stop in on Veronica. He would have liked to keep her informed, but knew if he went to her room, they would end up in bed. That would have to come later, when this was all over.

Chapter Thirty-Nine

In the morning Bat came to Clint's hotel, walking a horse he had rented. They had a quick breakfast, and then walked to the livery to collect Clint's Tobiano.

"He has a head start on us," Bat said. "We'll need some supplies."

"Just some coffee and jerky will do," Clint said. "We'll travel light so we can move fast."

They mounted their horses.

"A quick stop at the mercantile, and then we'll go," Clint said. "But Veronica—"

"I saw her this morning in the lobby," Bat said. "I explained what we're doing, and she said she'd wait."

"Let's go, then," Clint said.

***

After the stop at the mercantile, Clint picked up the tracks left by Tweedy's horse.

"See the mark?" he told Bat, as they both dismounted.

"I see it."

"He headed east," Clint said.

They mounted again and started in that direction.

"If Kenyon's involved, they must've met somewhere," Bat said. "Maybe to split the money."

"That would be good," Clint said. "Then he wouldn't be as far ahead of us."

As it turned out, they had some success after only a couple of hours. The tracks led to a small shack. When they reached it, Clint saw tracks from another horse.

"Okay," he told Bat, "they met up here."

"Let's take a look inside," Bat suggested.

Clint agreed. They went to the front door of the shack and opened it.

"Oh damn," Clint said.

They found Kenyon lying on the floor, dead of a stab wound.

"I guess Tweedy didn't want to split the take," Bat said.

"He's killed two people, already," Clint said.

"Where's he going?" Bat asked. "He must have a destination in mind."

"It'll have to be a long way off," Clint said. "He can't risk settling anywhere too near to Central City. He's going to have to leave Colorado."

"With that much money," Bat said, "he's likely to be going to New York to set himself up."

"But he can't think we wouldn't come after him," Clint said.

"All that way?" Bat asked.

"For that amount of money? I think so."

They left the shack.

"Two horses left," Bat said. "Even I can see that."

"He probably set Kenyon's horse free," Clint said. "Hoping someone would follow those tracks."

They mounted up and continued to follow Tweedy's tracks.

"See?" Clint said, after about a mile, "the other horse isn't with him."

"Do you think he'll stop in Denver?" Bat asked. "It's a big enough place for him to get lost."

"He might layover there," Clint said, "but I don't think he'll stay."

"If we come to a town with a telegraph, you could send a message to Talbot Roper."

"That's a good idea," Clint said.

They continued on for another few miles, and then Clint stopped when they crossed a stream.

"What is it?" Bat asked.

"He didn't come out of the stream here," Clint said. "I think he's following it to hide his tracks."

"Which way?" Bat asked.

"I'll follow it north, you follow it south. If you see his tracks come out, fire two shots. I'll do the same."

"Got it."

They separated. Clint hoped Tweedy wouldn't have followed the stream too far. He didn't want to get too far apart from Bat.

He followed the stream, watching for Tweedy's tracks to come out, and then something occurred to him. He retraced his steps, looking for tracks on the other side of the stream. Very quickly he found them. Tweedy had gone into the stream, followed it and then come out the same way. Clint drew his gun and fired two shots.

When Bat reached him, he was off his horse, letting the animal drink.

"Find him?" Bat asked.

"Not only did I find him," Clint said, pointing. "Look at this."

Bat dismounted and walked over to Clint, then looked at the ground.

"Is that right?" Bat asked.

"It's the same horse," Clint said. "It looks to me like Tweedy's doubling back to Central City."

"What the hell for?" Bat asked.

Clint looked at his friend and said, "Gloria."

Chapter Forty

When Gloria saw her husband at the back door, she threw her arms around him.

"I knew you wouldn't leave me behind," she said.

With his arms tightly around her he said, "I had to get them off my trail. Now you can pack, and we'll get out of here."

She drew him into the kitchen and closed the back door.

"Then it's true?" she asked.

"What's true?"

"You took that money?"

"That was the whole point of the challenge to get the money for us."

"But Clint Adams and Bat Masterson are not happy."

"I never expected the likes of them to sign up for this," he admitted, "but I had to go ahead with it. Now hurry. I've got one more thing to do and then I'll be back."

"My God, be careful out there."

"I will."

***

Tweedy entered the Blue Rose by the back door, made his way down a hall that left him behind the bar.

"Ike!" he hissed.

The man turned and looked at him in surprise.

"Hey, boss," Ike said. "I heard you were gone."

"Almost," Tweedy said. "I came back to tell you this place is yours now."

"You came back for that?"

"Well," Tweedy said, "among other things."

"So it's mine, just like that?" Ike asked.

"You'll find an envelope in my desk drawer," Tweedy said. "Inside is a document that gives this place to you."

"Well, thanks boss."

"And take this." He handed the man a bulging envelope.

"What is it?"

"Twenty thousand dollars," Tweedy said. "You'll have to pay the guards and the girls, but then the rest is yours."

"Did you hear about Call?" Ike asked.

"What about him?"

"He's dead," Ike said. "Somebody killed him in his bed."

"That could've been Kenyon," Tweedy said. "Don't worry about him."

"What about Adams and Masterson?" Ike asked. "They're lookin' for you."

"They won't find me. I left them a false trail to follow."

"I hope you're right, boss."

"What did you tell them?"

"Nothin'," Ike said. "I had nothin' to tell."

"Okay, keep it that way."

"How much longer are you gonna be in town?"

"Not long, but keep your mouth shut about it," Tweedy said.

"Sure, boss."

"I'm not the boss anymore," Tweedy said. "You are."

"Oh, right."

"Good luck, Ike," Tweedy said. "You won't see me again."

"S'long, bo— s'long, Wil."

Tweedy went back up the hall to the back door. When he stepped outside, he felt something in the small of his back.

"Hi, partner," Mattingly said. "Feel that?"

"I feel it," Tweedy said. "You been following me?"

"Naw," Mattingly said, "I've been watching your wife. When you left her, I followed you here. Thought you'd lost me?"

"I didn't lose you, you lost me," Tweedy said. "I was going to split with you and Kenyon."

"Kenyon, huh?" Mattingly said, digging his gun deeper into Tweedy's back. "What happened to him. The same thing that happened to your guard, Call?"

"Call had to go, he knew I'd been in the safe."

"Why didn't you just offer him a split, too?" Mattingly said. "You wouldn't have paid him, anyway."

"Now look—"

"You look. Take out your gun and hand it back to me, real easy."

Tweedy had a gun in a shoulder rig. He took it out and handed it back.

"Now let's go," Mattingly said. "Back to your house. The money's got to be there."

"Gloria's not in on this," Tweedy said.

"So she told me."

"What did you do to her?"

"Don't worry, she's fine," Mattingly said. "A little tied up, at the moment. But I need her to get to the money, so let's go."

"Look, the longer you make me stay in town Tweedy said, "the better chance there is of Adams, and Masterson catching up."

"Then we better move fast, don't you think?" He pushed the barrel of his gun into Tweedy's back hard enough to bruise it. "Move!"

"Okay, okay," Tweedy said, "I'm moving."

Chapter Forty-One

Clint and Bat pressed their horses, Clint's Tobiano taking the lead. They'd only been gone from Central City for about five hours, and they were riding back hell-bent-for-leather, which would cut that time in half. They were lucky Tweedy hadn't taken longer to lay his false trail.

Still, by the time they got back to town, Tweedy could be gone again. Even though he might have his wife with him, slowing him down, he would have a good head start, and they would have to start tracking him, again. And tracking someone slowed your pace considerably. So Clint was hoping that something—or maybe some-one—would keep Tweedy in town longer. Maybe his wife wouldn't want to go with him when she learned he was not only a thief, but a murderer, twice over.

It was obvious that Kenyon was a plant in the game. Maybe Tweedy was hoping the man would actually win, but when it was obvious he wasn't, the plan changed. They met at that shack, and Tweedy gave Kenyon a knife rather than a split. His saddlebags were probably stuffed with cash.

***

Mattingly pushed Tweedy through the back door of his house. Gloria was there, tied and gagged in a chair, her eyes bright with fright.

"Okay, Tweedy," Mattingly said, "where is it?"

"It's not here, Mattingly."

"Then where is it?"

"Oh, no," Tweedy said, "first you let Gloria go, then I'll give you the money."

"Not a chance," Mattingly said, "You ran out on me once, I'm not giving you the chance to buffalo me again." He cocked the hammer of the Colt in his hand, then pointed the gun at the trussed-up Gloria. "She goes first, then you."

"You do that you'll never see the money."

"Neither will you, my friend," Mattingly said. "What's it gonna be?"

"Yeah, okay," Tweedy said. "The money's in my saddlebags."

"Where are the saddlebags?"

"On my horse, of course," Tweedy said. "I've got two horses packed and ready to go for Gloria and me."

"That's good," Mattingly said, "because I'll only need one. Untie her and let's go."

***

Clint and Bat were approaching Central City, their horses almost blowing steam. They reined in for Clint to check the ground.

"Still there," he said. "He's definitely going back to Central City."

"He'd risk all that money for a woman," Bat said, shaking his head. "He must really love her."

"So she was right about him not leaving without her," Clint said. "At least we'll know where to look. Come on!"

They kicked their heels and headed to town at a gallop.

***

Mattingly pushed Tweedy and Gloria ahead of him. "Which stable?"

"The one owned by Buford Taylor."

"That don't mean nothing to me."

"South end of town," Tweedy said. "It's a bit of a walk."

"Stay off Main Street," Mattingly said.

"Yeah, sure," Tweedy said.

J.R. Roberts

***

Sheriff Wood was heading for a small café at the south end of Main Street, to get himself a meal, and then bring the prisoner something. He spotted Tweedy and Gloria being followed by another man. Since Tweedy was supposed to be missing, he stopped and watched. The man behind them had a gun.

He knew Clint Adams and Bat Masterson were out of town, and since he was wearing a badge, he didn't have much choice.

"Damn it to hell!" he breathed and followed them.

***

As they approached the livery stable, Mattingly gave Tweedy a hard shove to quicken his pace.

"There better not be anyone else in there," Mattingly snapped.

"I can't help that," Tweedy said. "Buford owns the place. He might be there."

"That'd be too bad for Buford."

"You'd just kill him, and us?" Tweedy asked.

Gloria grabbed his arm tightly.

"You never killed nobody?" Mattingly laughed.

Tweedy didn't answer.

They entered the livery stable.

178

Chapter Forty-Two

Sheriff Wood saw Tweedy and his wife led into the stable by the man with the gun. Since Tweedy had absconded with the money from the poker challenge, Wood had no choice but to step in. In the end, maybe there would be a reward for the return of the money.

He ran to the livery and stopped just outside the door to listen.

***

Inside the stable Mattingly said, "Okay, where's your horses?"

"The last two stalls on that side," Tweedy said, pointing.

"Show me."

They walked to the stalls, saw two horses, saddled and ready to go. One of them had bulging saddlebags.

"Well, whataya know," Mattingly said. "Get those saddlebags off." He pointed his gun at Gloria. "And remember, she gets the first bullet."

"Take it easy," Tweedy said. He stepped into the stall and removed both saddlebags. When he came out, he tossed them at Mattingly's feet. "There you go."

"Is it all there?"

"Every penny." He steeled himself to jump Mattingly when he bent for the bags.

***

Sheriff Wood heard Tweedy say, "Every penny," and decided to step in at that moment. He drew his gun and moved.

"Hold it!" he hollered.

All three turned to look, and Mattingly brought his gun around. He fired, and the bullet hit the lawman dead center in the chest.

Tweedy took the opportunity to jump Mattingly and they tumbled to the ground.

"Wilford!" Gloria shouted.

The two men rolled on the ground, fighting for a superior position. Mattingly was holding fast to his gun.

Gloria watched for several seconds, then ran to the fallen sheriff and picked up his gun. Tweedy and Mattingly were still locked together, and she couldn't get a clear shot. But at that point, Mattingly attained a position atop Tweedy. She ran forward, and practically pressed the gun barrel to his head. When she fired, she also screamed.

Mattingly immediately collapsed dead atop Tweedy. He pushed the body off of himself and jumped to his feet.

Gloria stood there, the gun still in her hand, staring down at the dead man. She had never killed anyone before and was in shock. The gun in her hand was trembling.

Tweedy stepped to her and gently pried the gun from her grip, then took her into his arms.

"Easy now," he said, "easy."

"Oh my God," she gushed. "Oh God, I killed him." She looked up at her husband's face. "I killed him, Wil!"

"You had no choice," he told her. "He would've killed us both." He looked over at the sheriff. "Is he dead?"

"I—I don't know. I just picked up his gun."

"And good thing you did, too."

He released her and walked over to the fallen lawman and leaned over to check him.

"He's dead," he said. "He picked the wrong day to act like a real lawman."

He looked at his wife, who was still staring down at Mattingly's body. There was a pool of blood around his head.

"Okay," he said to her, "stop looking at him."

"I-I c-can't," she stuttered.

Tweedy went to her again and forcibly turned her around.

"That's it. Don't look."

When he released her, she remained facing away from the body.

"Just wait here."

"What are you going to do? Bury them?"

"We don't have time."

"Hide them, then?"

"There's no telling if anyone heard the shots," Tweedy said. "We have to move."

He picked up the saddlebags and tossed them back onto his horse, then walked both animals out of the stall.

"Come on!" He snapped at her and continued to lead the horses right out of the stable, walking around the sheriff's body. Gloria stumbled along behind him.

"Here you go," he said, grabbing her arm and pulling her to her horse. She had dressed in trousers and boots, ready to ride. He helped her up into the saddle.

"All right?" he asked.

"Y-yes, Wil."

"Wait here."

He went back into the stable, picked up his gun, and grabbed Mattingly's for good measure. He put his gun back in his shoulder rig, and tucked Mattingly's colt into his belt. Then went back outside, where he walked to his own horse and mounted up.

"Let's go!"

Chapter Forty-Three

When Clint and Bat rode into town, there was a flurry of activity going on.

"Damn it!" Clint swore.

"May not have anything to do with Tweedy," Bat said.

"That's too much to hope for," Clint replied.

They reined in and dismounted, grabbed ahold of a man going by.

"What's going on?" Clint asked.

"A shooting," the man said. "Somebody killed the sheriff."

"Any idea who did it?" Bat asked.

"There's another fella got shot, but nobody knows 'im."

"Where are the bodies?" Clint asked.

"The undertaker."

"Thanks," Clint said.

They walked their horses to the undertaker's shop. They tied off their horses and went inside. A tall, thin man wearing a dirty apron came into the room.

"Can I help you gents?" he asked.

"The sheriff and the other man who were shot," Bat said. "We want to see them."

"I don't know if I can do that."

"Look," Bat said, "I'm Bat Masterson and this is Clint Adams. Your sheriff was shot, and until you get another, we're all you have. Now let us see the bodies, and maybe we can catch whoever did it."

"Oh, w-well, certainly. In the back. This way."

He led them to a room where two bodies lay on tables. One was Sheriff Wood, shot in the chest. The other was Mattingly, who had been shot in the head.

"Did anyone see anything?" Clint asked. "Did they shoot each other?"

"One witness saw a man and a woman riding away soon after the shooting," the undertaker said.

"That's it," Clint said. "Tweedy and Gloria."

"When did all this happen?" Bat asked the undertaker.

"About an hour ago."

"Has anybody gone after them?" Clint asked.

"The mayor is going to appoint a new sheriff, but nothing's happened, yet."

"Which way did they go?" Bat asked.

"Not east, that's for sure," Clint said. "We came that way."

"They were seen riding west," the undertaker said, "but who knows which direction they went when they got out of town."

"We'll know," Clint said, "as soon as I pick up their trail."

"If Tweedy's riding the same horse," Bat said.

"We just need to find the fresh tracks of two animals," Clint said. "Once we know what direction they're going, we can run them down."

"You hope," Bat said.

"I think," Clint said, "Tweedy's got to ride at his wife's pace. We're sure to run them down. Come on."

"Not even time for a beer," Bat said, shaking his head.

"Whoever gets appointed sheriff," Clint said to the undertaker, "tell them where we went."

"Yes, sir."

Clint and Bat left the shop, mounted their horses, and rode west.

***

Outside of town they found the tracks. It looked like Tweedy had the same horse.

"They're going west, so far," Clint said. "Somewhere along the way they could change direction."

"If you wanted to start a new life with your woman, and you had all that money," Bat said, "where would you go?"

"That's easy," Clint said. "California."

"So they'll keep heading west."

"If we ride hard, we'll catch them," Clint said.

"Your horse might keep up that pace, but I don't know mine will."

"If we come to a ranch or another town, we'll get you a fresh mount."

"Then we might as well get going," Bat said.

***

Tweedy reined in to give Gloria a rest. It was the third time.

"Where are we going?" she asked, trying to catch her breath.

"Ultimately, California," Tweedy said. "But we'll stop somewhere along the way."

"When?"

"When we get far enough away from Central City," Tweedy said. "Preferably out of Colorado."

"Then what?"

"Then we'll decide which part of California we want to settle in."

"Won't they send someone after us?"

"They might, but first they'll have to appoint a new sheriff. By the time they do, and he sets out after us, we'll be out of their jurisdiction."

"But a lawman was killed," Gloria said. "Won't that justify them leaving their jurisdiction?"

"It might, but you forget, we didn't kill him, Mattingly did. And they have his body, as well. That might satisfy them."

"But will it satisfy Clint Adams and Bat Masterson?"

"They have no authority."

"Do they need it?" Gloria said. "Isn't killing people what they do?"

"When we get settled, we'll have enough money to hire security," Tweedy said. "If they find us, we'll handle them."

"You sound very confident."

"I am," Tweedy said. "I figured out every aspect of this. Mattingly almost ruined it, but he's dead."

"He insinuated you killed someone."

"He was trying to blame me for his actions," Tweedy said.

"And what happened to Kenyon?"

"Mattingly killed him," Tweedy said, "as well as one of my guards."

"He was a horrible man."

"Yes, he was. Can you go on?"

"Yes."

"We still have a little daylight, and then we'll camp for the night."

"I won't need to stop again until we camp," she said.

"Good. Let's move."

Chapter Forty-Four

Clint and Bat rode hard, stopping only to make sure they were still following the tracks. They did come to a ranch where they were able to buy a new horse for cash and a trade-in of Bat's mount. The Tobiano was still keeping up the pace.

When they reined in again to check the tracks, Bat said, "It'll be dark soon. We'll have to make camp."

"I was thinking of riding at night."

"That's taking a chance one of the horses might go lame."

"I realize that, but Tweedy and Gloria will camp for the night. If we keep going, we'll catch them."

"Okay, as long as you and your sure-footed horse take the lead, I'll follow along."

***

They continued for a couple of hours after dark, and before long Clint reined in.

"You smell that?" Clint asked.

Bat sniffed the air and said, "Coffee."

"Up ahead," Clint said. "Let's dismount and go on foot."

They stepped down, tied their horses off, and started walking.

After a few minutes Clint held his hand up, then pointed ahead. In the dark they could see the flickering light of a campfire.

"It might not be them," Clint whispered, "but that'd be a hell of a coincidence."

"So we don't go in shooting," Bat said.

"We want to take him and the money back to Central City," Clint reminded him.

"I may want to shoot the bastard," Bat said, "but I won't."

"I know what you mean," Clint said, "but good."

They started forward again, stepping as carefully as they could to be quiet. Before long they heard the voices of a man and a woman. The camp was just ahead of them. Clint motioned to Bat to go around to the other side. He said he would count to ten, and then go in. Bat nodded and faded into the darkness. He was dressed in dark clothes, but had left his bowler hat and stick behind.

Clint counted to ten slowly, then stepped out into the camp light. At the same time, Bat stepped from the other side. When Tweedy saw Clint, he started for his gun.

"Don't, Tweedy!" Clint snapped. "You'll never make it."

Gloria was seated at the fire and remained there, frozen.

"Don't kill him!" she cried.

"That'll be up to him, Ma'am," Bat said.

Clint's gun was holstered, but Bat was holding his. Tweedy spread his hands apart, away from his gun.

"Gloria, I'm going to ask you to take that gun from his shoulder rig with only two fingers and hand it to me."

"Go ahead, Gloria," Tweedy said, "do as he says."

She got to her feet, slowly walked to her husband and took his gun. When she turned to Clint, she held the gun out in front of her with two fingers. She walked to Clint and handed it to him.

"What are you going to do?" she asked.

"We're going to take both of you back to Central City, with the money."

"That's a lot of money, Clint, Bat," Tweedy said. "We could split it three ways."

"That doesn't suit me," Clint said. "Bat?"

"I don't think so."

"So I'll take my original cut and the rest is yours," Tweedy said.

Bat laughed. "That comes out to the same offer you just made."

"There are also some killings you have to answer for, Tweedy," Clint said.

"What killings?"

"Eddie Call, Kenyon, Mattingly, and Sheriff Woods."

"My husband didn't kill those men," Gloria said.

"That remains to be seen, Gloria," Clint said. "I think a jury's going to decide that."

"B-but, Mattingly shot the sheriff and I—I shot Mattingly," she confessed.

"Even if that's true, there are still Call and Kenyon," Clint said.

"But why would he kill his own man, or Kenyon?"

"Call knew he took the money from the safe, and Kenyon . . . well, he was supposed to get a cut, so your husband killed him, instead," Clint said. "At least, that's how I figure it. But like I said, it'll be up to a jury."

"So what do we do now?" Tweedy asked.

"We tie you up, and sit around the fire until morning," Clint said.

"I'll go get the horses and bring them in," Bat said.

"Take Gloria with you, Bat," Clint said. "I think we're better off keeping them apart."

"Good idea. Come on, Gloria."

Gloria looked at Clint and said, "You're not going to kill him, are you?"

"No, Ma'am," Clint said. "There are too many people back in Central City waiting to see him."

"We'll be right back with the horses," Bat said, and he and Gloria left the camp.

Chapter Forty-Five

Clint tied Tweedy's hands behind him and sat him by the fire, then settled across from him.

"Okay, Tweedy it's just you and me. What was the setup?"

Clint was surprised when Tweedy readily answered.

"It was a sweet deal, really," he said. "Both Kenyon and Mattingly were good poker players. I was hoping one of them would win, and maybe the other would come in second, and I'd end up with most of the money. But I didn't expect you, and Masterson, and Lady Poker to show up. When the game came down to you three and Kenyon,I figured the jig was up."

"So you came up with that break for supper?"

"Right."

"And that's why Kenyon didn't eat with us, because you and him took off with the money. He thought you were going to split it when you got to that shack."

"It's too much damn money to split," Tweedy said. "I had to get rid of Call first, because he was in for a small piece for looking the other way while I opened the safe."

"And you didn't want to even give up a small piece."

"Like I said, it's too much to split."

"What about Mattingly?"

"He pulled a gun, and was trying to take the whole caboodle. The sheriff stepped in and saved my ass. Mattingly shot him, we tussled for his gun, but Gloria shot him, like she said."

"And that left you and Gloria."

"That's the way it was supposed to be from the start."

At that point Bat and Gloria arrived with the horses. Bat unsaddled them and picketed them with Tweedy's animal, then came to the fire.

"Coffee?" he said.

"I made some," Gloria said.

"I'll pour it," Bat said, "just so you don't get any ideas."

He poured a cup for him and Clint. Gloria sat at the fire. They tied her hands but left them in front of her.

"What are you going to do with the money when we get back?" Tweedy asked.

"Not sure," Clint said. "Doesn't seem fair for me and Bat to split it. Veronica and Johnny should probably get some."

"Why?" Tweedy asked. "Kenyon's dead, and you and Bat are left. Go ahead and split it."

"You bamboozled a lot of people, Tweedy," Bat said. "They should probably all get their buy-in back."

"How the hell would you find all of them to do that?" Tweedy asked.

"We could put the money in the Central City bank," Clint said, "and send out word. Players could come back in whenever they could and pick it up."

"There's a lot to discuss," Bat said. "You got anything to eat?"

***

Later, after they had made some beans, Tweedy and Gloria fell asleep. They sat at the fire with the saddlebags of cash at their feet.

"Too bad he didn't resist," Bat said. "I would like to have plugged him."

"It would have made things easier," Clint said.

"He's right, you know," Bat said. "We can't possibly get the money back to all the players."

"Veronica will still be in town when we get back," Clint said. "You want to do a three-way split?"

"I think Veronica should get the money she won," Bat said.

"Ok, then that leaves you and me to split the rest." Clint said.

"Sounds fair to me," Bat said. "We didn't steal anything, that was Tweedy. We probably would've come in first and second, anyway. And what about Tweedy's original cut?"

"We've got time to think about it on the way back," Clint said.

"Yeah, we do," Bat agreed.